WHEN I WAS A GIRL, I USED TO SCREAM AND SHOUT . . .

with

WHEN WE WERE WOMEN

and

THE BRAVE

Sharman Macdonald

faber and faber

LONDON · BOSTON

This collection first published in 1990
by Faber and Faber Limited
3 Queen Square London WC1N 3AU

Photoset by Wilmaset Birkenhead Wirral
Printed in Great Britain by
Richard Clay Ltd Bungay Suffolk

Sharman Macdonald is hereby identified as author of
this work in accordance with Section 77 of the
Copyright, Designs and Patents Act 1988.

The publisher acknowledges with gratitude financial
subsidy from the Scottish Arts Council towards
the publication of this volume.

All professional and amateur rights in these plays
are strictly reserved and applications for permission
to perform them must be made in advance to
MacNaughton Lowe Representation Ltd,
200 Fulham Road, London SW10.

A CIP record for this book is
available from the British Library.

ISBN 0-571-14348-2

To Will Knightley

CONTENTS

WHEN I WAS A GIRL, I USED
TO SCREAM AND SHOUT . . .

CHARACTERS

MORAG   The mother
FIONA   The daughter
VARI   The friend
EWAN   The boyfriend

The play takes place on a rocky beach on the east coast of
Scotland. The set is on two levels. Above is part of a prom, a
street light and a railing. Below, a tunnel leads through the
façade of the prom to the rocks. Cut into the rocks is a small
swimming pool about 4 feet square and waist-height.

When I Was a Girl, I Used to Scream and Shout . . . was first performed at the Bush Theatre, London, in November 1984. The cast was as follows:

MORAG   Sheila Reid
FIONA   Eleanor David
VARI   Celia Imrie
EWAN   John Gordon Sinclair

Director   Simon Stokes
Designer   Robin Don
Music   Richard Brown
Lighting   Paul Denby

ACT ONE

SCENE I

1983
The beach.
FIONA *is lying on a towel in a bikini, sunbathing.* MORAG *is sitting on a travelling rug, surrounded by bags.*

MORAG: I'm not dressed up. I bought this years ago. Marks and Spencer's. It's a cheap summer dress. It's a nice dress, but it's only cheap. You feel the material. Come on over here and have a feel of this.
(FIONA *gets up.*)
Away and don't bother your head. I wouldn't dress up to come down on a beach. I know beaches. All right, these are new. I bought a new pair of sandals to come away for the weekend. What's wrong with that? It's my own wee treat. I'm generous enough with you. I like to look nice. What's wrong with that? I've been well groomed all my life. I'll not stop now. Not even for you. I'll be smart if I want, but as for dressed up . . . What's wrong with you?
FIONA: I said, 'You're all dressed up.' I was smiling.
MORAG: I brought you on this weekend.
FIONA: I'm very grateful.
MORAG: I wanted to see my roses.
FIONA: They're not your roses.
MORAG: I planted them. I tended them. I loved them. But for me there'd be no roses. That house can change hands umpteen times. Those roses are my roses.
FIONA: All right, they're . . .
MORAG: A wee holiday.
FIONA: Mum . . .
MORAG: You can say, 'You're all dressed up', or you can say, 'You're all dressed up.'
FIONA: You look very smart.
MORAG: We could have a nice time together. A nice quiet time.
FIONA: The colour suits you.

5

MORAG: Horse dung, cow dung. I manured those roses with my own hands. All 200 of them. That display is mine.

FIONA: It's beautiful.

MORAG: I thought a nice weekend back here. I've something for you.

FIONA: You shouldn't go on spending money.

MORAG: I mean, if you'd said, 'You're all dressed up.'

FIONA: It's a nice dress.

MORAG: No man, no child, no money. I don't like to see you like this.

FIONA: I'm not that bad.

MORAG: I want to bring the brightness back to your eyes. Here. Come here. Come and see.
(*She brings out a coral necklace.* FIONA *gets up and goes to the travelling rug.*)

FIONA: These rocks are burning.

MORAG: Come on to the travelling rug.

FIONA: I'm fine.

MORAG: You'll burn your bum.

FIONA: I'm all right.

MORAG: Oh, well then. Here. This was yours when you were wee. I had a new clasp put on it. It's coral. Here.
(*She fastens it round* FIONA's *neck and hands her a mirror.*)
What do you think? Of course, it's right in the fashion. You get some colour in your skin.

FIONA: It's lovely.

MORAG: You need a man to give you gold. A gold chain lying with that. You've fine skin. Takes me back. That lying round your neck. Do you want a cup of coffee? I've plenty coffee.

FIONA: No.

MORAG: All those years ago and that lying round your chubby wee neck. Fatty, fatty, fatty but awful bonny. I'm going to have some. (*Pours.*) See that necklace? I was keeping that for my first grandchild.

FIONA: You've got a grandchild.

MORAG: That doesn't count.

FIONA: Don't be daft.

6

MORAG: I never held him. I never saw him. I mean a proper
    child. Of my body. Of your body. You're thirty-two,
    Fiona. A wee head to hold in my hand. A wee head, Fiona.
    A wee head to hold in my hand.

FIONA: Did you bring me here for this?

MORAG: You're not showing your age.

FIONA: Did you?

MORAG: You'll burn your bum on those rocks.

FIONA: Am I to have a whole weekend of this?

MORAG: Your Auntie Nellie had the menopause at thirty. Are
    you going to tell me you're happy? You've not even got a
    man. Come on to the rug.

FIONA: No.

MORAG: Every woman needs to have a child. I remember the
    day I could wear necklaces. You've my neck. I had a good
    neck. When I was thirty-two, you were five. A woman's
    body is a clock that runs down very rapidly. You don't
    need me to tell you that.

FIONA: You survived without a man.

MORAG: Did I? I'm here, that's all you can say. I've loved you
    all your life. Fiona. No matter what you've done. A wee
    child to hold in my arms. From your body. From my body.
    A wee child at my knee.

    (*A voice from inside the swimming pool –*)

VARI: Hey.

FIONA: Christ.

MORAG: I told her you'd be here.

FIONA: Thanks.

MORAG: Away on over with you.

    (FIONA *goes over to the pool.*)

1955
The bedroom.

VARI: Willie games?

FIONA: She'll see.

VARI: Not down here.

FIONA: Pencils?

VARI: Pencils. (*She holds up two.*)

FIONA: Pram covers?

VARI: Two fluffy ones with bunny rabbits.

FIONA: Excellent.

VARI: Willie games?

FIONA: Yes.

VARI: You come in.

FIONA: (*Jumps in*) You first.

VARI: I was walking along the road, doctor, and I suddenly realized it wasn't there. I've only got a hole. My penis must have dropped off. Can you help me?

FIONA: It'll be very sore.

VARI: I need my penis back, doctor.

FIONA: There's been a great demand this morning. You can have a red penis or a blue penis.

VARI: Blue, please.

FIONA: Lie down.

VARI: Can you find the hole?

FIONA: It's huge. This'll hurt. You say, 'Ouch.'

VARI: Ouch.

FIONA: That's the operation over.

VARI: You've kind hands, doctor.

FIONA: Thank you.

VARI: I'll need a bandage.

FIONA: I've a nice fluffy one here.

VARI: I like rabbits.

FIONA: There.

VARI: Oh, doctor, will my new penis take?

FIONA: We'll know that tomorrow.

VARI: Now you.

FIONA: Oh, doctor, I kept wetting the bed and my Mummy said if I didn't stop she'd cut it off. Well, I didn't stop so she did cut it off and it hurt a lot, a lot, a lot. Now I don't wet the bed any more can I have a new penis, please?

VARI: You're very lucky I've got one left.

FIONA: What colour is it?

VARI: Red.

FIONA: That'll do nicely, thank you.

VARI: Lie down.

FIONA: I'm not playing.

VARI: I did, you have to.

FIONA: I don't want a pencil stuck up me.

VARI: It's a penis and I've got one stuck up me. And if it takes
I'll be a boy and you won't.

(FIONA *gets out of the pool.* VARI *follows.*)

1983
The beach.

FIONA: You were a bloody Queen's Guide. Badges crawling up
your arms. The Duke of Edinburgh skulking at your
elbow. You made me sick. Always making lemon curd and
doing the dusting. You told me there was no Santa Claus. I
was sucking a gobstopper. I had just started it. I swallowed
it whole. It yo-yoed up and down inside me for days. Cause
as soon as you said it I knew it was true. There's no Santa
Claus.

VARI: So what?

FIONA: Waste of a good gobstopper.

MORAG: What's that bumfle under your skirt, Vari?

VARI: Just keeping warm, Auntie Morag.

MORAG: Never let yourself go, Vari. No matter how tired you
are. No matter how depressed you are, you can always have
your hair nice and your clothes well brushed. And a bit of
lipstick won't break the bank. If your lips look like they'll
take a kiss things won't go far wrong. You've put on
weight.

VARI: I'm always hungry.

MORAG: How many is it now?

VARI: Three.

MORAG: What age?

VARI: Four, three and eight months.

MORAG: I've something for them. I've three silver bracelets
here. They used to be Fiona's. Silver's awful pretty on a
baby's skin. You take these. Fiona always had a silver
bracelet. I was keeping these for my first grandchild but
we're out of luck. Fiona's Auntie Nellie, well, her Great

9

Auntie, my Auntie that was, Auntie Nellie had the
menopause at thirty.

FIONA: I had a baby.

MORAG: At least we know you're fertile.

VARI: They're lovely. The girls'll be delighted. Thank you very
much.

MORAG: You've not been a mother. You're a sad woman. Look
at your eyes.

VARI: Look at mine, Auntie Morag, I don't get a night's sleep.

MORAG: I've a nice cup of tea here. 'The old Bohea,' Fiona's
Great Aunt Jean used to say. Her that was Auntie Nellie's
sister.

FIONA: The bracelets dug into my arm.

MORAG: When you come down to the beach you've got to be
prepared. I bring coffee, tea, sandwiches and cake. And of
course the odd bit of fruit and a biscuit or two. I know
beaches. (*She begins to lay out a picnic.*)

VARI: What have you come here for?

MORAG: All the sandwiches are on brown bread. I insist on
that. I'm not a faddy eater but brown bread is a must in my
eyes. Of course Fiona's a vegetarian. So difficult at the
hotel.

FIONA: We came because she wanted to.

MORAG: And she doesn't like eggs.

VARI: What for?

MORAG: There's so much nonsense talked about food. Health
this and whole that. Fiona's Great Auntie Nellie lived till
she was ninety and her favourite food was rare steak
covered in cream. Will you have a corned-beef sandwich?

VARI: Thank you.

MORAG: Of course she lost all her hair with the menopause. I've
cheese and tomato for you. Apart from that she was
healthy.

FIONA: No, thank you.

MORAG: You take it. I'll not see you scraggy. I can count your
ribs. A man likes a bit of flesh to puddle his fingers in.
Vari's three children are the living proof of that. Hours
you'd spend in that bedroom. I could always trust you two

to play together. Not like boys. Always with their hands on their dirty wee things. Do you take sugar?

VARI: Two, please.

MORAG: Another sandwich?

VARI: Yes, please.

MORAG: Have you thought of joining the Weight Watchers?

VARI: I'm always like this when I'm feeding.

MORAG: Three children. You'll never be lonely. Be a good daughter to your mother and your children'll do good by you. Eat your sandwich, Fiona, you look drawn.

FIONA: You don't look well, Fiona. We're none of us getting any younger, Fiona. You've bags under your eyes, you've wrinkles in your forehead, your wee bit breasts are sagging. Child, menopause, child. It's a mother's place to worry. What else am I going to do? I've all my eggs in the one basket. I didn't want to come back here. What do you want to come back here for?

MORAG: It was a good place to live.

FIONA: If you've something to say to me will you not just say it?

MORAG: I've lived without a man these past seventeen years. I'm lonely. I want a grandchild.

(*Silence.*)

VARI: These are lovely sandwiches.

MORAG: I'd say that was my right.

FIONA: It is not.

MORAG: What did I give birth to you for?

VARI: Could I maybe have another cup of tea?

MORAG: Come on to the rug, you'll burn your bum.

(FIONA *goes to the pool and gets in.* VARI *follows.*)

1959
The bathroom.

VARI: Do you know where babies come from?

FIONA: Up your Auntie Mary. Down the plug-hole.

VARI: Do you know how they get in there?

FIONA: A woman has a period and a man has a period, sort of, and if they coincide and they happen to be touching, if

they're married and they're in bed together then the
woman gets a baby.

VARI: How do you know that?

FIONA: I just do.

VARI: See when you get your doings you have to be very
careful. I mean if a man touches you then, even if a finger
of a man touches you, you might get pregnant.

FIONA: My Daddy?

VARI: You'll have to keep him off.

FIONA: Girls don't get pregnant to their fathers.

VARI: Girls are careful. After you've got your doings every time
you have a big job, you know the hard kind you have to
press out, you mind and look behind you. There might be
a baby swimming about there down the bog in amongst the
jobbies. So don't pull the flush too quick.

FIONA: What else am I going to do with it?

VARI: You'd have to love it and take care of it.

FIONA: I'm not putting my hand down there to fish it out.

VARI: Your Mum likes babies.

FIONA: She'd be cross. She's very bad-tempered, my Mum.
She'd think I'd been careless.

VARI: You'd just have to break it to her gently.

FIONA: I think I'd rather pull the flush.

VARI: You're disgusting.

FIONA: Well, what would you do?

VARI: My Mum says always to remember that whatever I do,
she'd always love me so never be afraid to tell her anything
cause she'd take care of me.

FIONA: My Mum said that too.

VARI: They're talking about babies.

FIONA: I still think they'd be cross.

VARI: You've got hairs.

FIONA: Where?

VARI: Down there. Look.

FIONA: Oh, yes. They're nice.

VARI: I haven't got any.

FIONA: There's six. Daddy, Daddy.

(VARI *puts her hand over* FIONA's *mouth.*)

12

VARI: Let me get out first.

FIONA: Daddy, Daddy, Daddy, Daddy, Daddy, Daddy.

(MORAG *jumps up and runs over.*)

MORAG: What is it? What is it?

FIONA: I've got hair. I've got six hairs. Go and get Daddy.

MORAG: I thought you'd gone down the plug-hole. The fuss.

FIONA: Get Daddy. Get Daddy.

MORAG: What do you want him for?

FIONA: I want him to see. Have I got breasts? Look, I've got
bumps. Go and get Daddy.

MORAG: You can't have your father in the bathroom.

FIONA: Why not?

MORAG: You're very nearly a young lady.

FIONA: He'd like to see my hairs.

MORAG: You must always have your clothes on when you see
your Father.

FIONA: But my hairs.

MORAG: I'll tell him.

FIONA: You haven't looked.

MORAG: Very nice.

FIONA: They're black. Did you see? Did you? Soon it'll be a
forest. That'll be nice. Dorothy hasn't got hair and she's
older than me. She says she used to have breasts but
they've gone down to get more skin so that they can come
back up again.

MORAG: You're to stop asking your Father to tickle your
tummy on a Saturday morning.

FIONA: He likes it.

MORAG: You'll have your doings soon. You'll be a young lady.
That'll make Gran proud. Daddies don't tickle the tummies
of young ladies.

FIONA: You've not to tell Gran. Who'll tickle my tummy? I
need my tummy tickled. Don't tell Gran. Promise. I don't
want to be a young lady.

MORAG: It can be the curse indeed.

FIONA: I've just got hairs. Don't tell. Don't tell anyone. No
one's to know. It'll be a secret, you and me. If I get breasts
I'll cross my arms and no one'll know.

MORAG: We're not great ones for breasts in our family.

FIONA: If I don't have them no man'll ever want me.

MORAG: I did all right. You're a very pretty girl and don't let anyone tell you other. Now. Out of the bath and straight to bed.

(FIONA *stands up.* MORAG *wraps her in a towel and bustles her to the sunbathing area.* FIONA *lies down.*)

1960
The bedroom.

MORAG: One story, that's all.

FIONA: Two.

MORAG: One, then sleep.

FIONA: Two.

MORAG: We'll see.

FIONA: Please. Please.

MORAG: One.

FIONA: Two.

MORAG: Move over.

(FIONA *wriggles her bum to take up all the towel.*)

Move or I'll go downstairs.

(FIONA *doesn't move.* MORAG *sets off for the tunnel.*)

FIONA: I've moved. Don't go. I've moved. I've moved.

(MORAG *comes back and begins to settle herself beside her daughter on the towel.* FIONA *is wriggling.*)

MORAG: What are you doing?

FIONA: Jigging.

MORAG: Keep still.

FIONA: Why?

MORAG: How jigging?

FIONA: Like this.

MORAG: What's it for?

FIONA: Makes me sleepy.

MORAG: Why?

FIONA: Feels nice.

MORAG: I see.

FIONA: Tell me a story.

MORAG: How nice?

FIONA: You know.

MORAG: I'm hoping I don't know. I'm hoping that you're my own good girl. Are you?

FIONA: Yes.

MORAG: I'm glad. Where does it feel nice?

FIONA: Inside.

MORAG: Where inside?

FIONA: Between my legs and up a bit.

MORAG: It's a bad thing you're doing.

FIONA: It makes me sleepy.

MORAG: I couldn't tell Daddy you were doing this.

FIONA: Why?

MORAG: Now you know there's a God upstairs and he looks down and he sees everything you do.

FIONA: I'll only do it in the dark.

MORAG: God can see in the dark. He sees everything and everyone and if he spots wee Fiona jigging in her bed in the dark, do you know what he does? Do you?

FIONA: What does he do?

MORAG: He looks down and he says to himself, 'That wee Fiona's a naughty, naughty girl and I thought she was one of my better efforts. That wee Fiona's jigging. Tttt. Tttt. Tttt,' he goes. And he calls the Recording Angel. And he says to the Recording Angel, 'I put wee Fiona on the earth to make her mummy happy and look at her now. Jigging. Recording Angel,' says God and the Recording Angel says, 'Yes, Lord.' 'Recording Angel,' says God, 'take up your pen' and the Recording Angel, who's always crying for he has a very sad job, takes up his great big feather pen with the sharp point. 'Recording Angel,' says God, 'open up the book and dip the pen.' The Recording Angel opens the big red book that hangs from his waist by a chain and dips his pen in God's great big inkwell. 'Find wee Fiona's name,' says God and he looks down in his infinite kindness to give you one more chance but you're still jigging away down there in the dark and God blushes for the shame of it and the Recording Angel's tears fall all the faster. And God says, 'Put a black mark at wee Fiona's name, she's a

disappointment to me' and the Recording Angel puts a big
black mark at your name. And do you know what happens
if you get enough black marks? Do you, Fiona?

FIONA: No.

MORAG: You don't go to heaven to pick the flowers in God's
green meadows when you die. God casts you down. He
looks in his big book and he sees all the black marks. He
says, 'I don't want wee Fiona here to dirty up my nice
heaven' and he sends you down, all the way down to the
devil who's like a snake only worse and the devil sticks you
on a spit and roasts you in the fires of hell so he can eat you
for dinner.

FIONA: Does it hurt?

MORAG: Oh, yes, it hurts a lot.

FIONA: For jigging?

MORAG: That's right.

FIONA: If I stop now do you think God'll say it's all right?

MORAG: I'm sure he'll be very proud of you.

FIONA: I won't do it any more.

MORAG: That's my good girl. Mummy loves you very much.
Mummy will always love you whatever you do.

FIONA: What about God?

MORAG: I'll have a word. Good night. Sleep tight. Don't let the
bugs bite.

(MORAG *goes.* VARI *comes over surreptitiously from the
swimming pool and crouches by* FIONA's *head.*)

1961
The bedroom.

VARI: She's got it all wrong.

FIONA: What?

VARI: There's no God.

FIONA: Yes, there is.

VARI: No, there isn't.

FIONA: Yes, there is.

VARI: I was right about Santa Claus.

FIONA: Does that mean it's all right to do it?

VARI: No.

FIONA: Why?

VARI: If you do that your husband'll know when you get married and he'll despise you.

FIONA: How will he know? You can't see.

VARI: If you keep doing it you go all hard inside. You go like concrete and he can't get in to get his pleasure. So he knows.

FIONA: Why does he want to get in?

VARI: His penis needs to. It sort of gets up and leads him to the hole and it tries to get in and if it can't the man knows it's your fault and you get divorced. He knows you've been dirty and no man'll live with a dirty lady. He shouldn't be expected to, my Mum says.

FIONA: Are you sure his penis goes in?

VARI: I've seen.

FIONA: Oh, well.

VARI: Do you want me to tell you?

FIONA: I think I've had enough for one night.

VARI: What're you lying all scrunched up for?

FIONA: I've got snakes in the bed. They're all round me and I've only got this tiny space to lie in.

VARI: That's not very nice.

FIONA: They're under the bed too and there's bugs on the wall. But there's a gun where the door handle used to be and if I can reach that I'll be all right.

VARI: Did you know your Mum and Dad were getting divorced?

FIONA: Is there still a Jesus?

VARI: Seems to be proof of that.

FIONA: That's nice.

VARI: Did you hear me?

FIONA: My Mum and Dad are getting divorced. (*Pause.*) Has she gone all hard inside?

VARI: He's got another woman. Who can blame him, my Mum says. Do you believe me?

FIONA: Yes. What about me?

VARI: My Mum says you've been a bit of a disappointment. My

Mum says your Father didn't want a child and your Mum tricked him to get you. Said it was safe when it wasn't.

FIONA: My Mum must love me then.

VARI: Suppose she must. She won't like her man going though, my Mum says, it's a terrible stigma.

FIONA: Are you sure about Jesus?

VARI: Oh, yes.

FIONA: Does he live in the sky?

VARI: He's dead.

FIONA: There's not a lot of point in that then.

VARI: What?

FIONA: I thought he might help with my Mum and Dad.

VARI: No chance.

FIONA: I'm going to sleep now.

VARI: In the dark. I'm scared of the dark.

FIONA: So am I.

VARI: There's bogies in the dark.

FIONA: I know.

VARI: They'll get you.

FIONA: I know.

VARI: We could both get in together, then we'd be all right.

FIONA: What do you mean?

VARI: I could get in with you. You're awful thick sometimes.

FIONA: Why?

VARI: Bogies don't attack you when you're with someone.

FIONA: Why not?

VARI: Never mind why not. They don't, that's all. But if you want the bogies to get you, that's your tough tof.

FIONA: OK then.

VARI: OK then what?

FIONA: Get in.

VARI: I don't know if I want to now.

FIONA: Och, Vari, come on.

VARI: Bogies cling to the wall and drop on your face and they suffocate you. It's a horrible death, my Mum says.

FIONA: Gonnie get in?

VARI: Say 'Please'.

FIONA: Please.

VARI: Move, then. (VARI *gets into the towel bed*.) Are you sure
    there's snakes in here?

FIONA: Yes.

VARI: I can't feel them.

FIONA: They're only here for me.

VARI: Right, I'm comfy.

FIONA: Good.

VARI: I've an idea.

FIONA: What?

VARI: Do you want to know what it's like when a man and
    woman do it?

FIONA: Eh?

VARI: Do you?

FIONA: What, now?

VARI: Why not?

FIONA: How?

VARI: I'll be the man and you be the woman.

FIONA: What do I do?

VARI: Take your jammies off.

FIONA: I will not.

VARI: Shhhhh. Shhhhh. Do you want everyone to hear? It's
    only sensible to practise. We've got to make it as real as
    possible. I mean, you don't think they do it with their
    clothes on, do you?

FIONA: I don't know.

VARI: Well, they don't. It's only sensible. How can his thing go
    in you if you've got a pair of pyjamas in the way? That's
    what's known as contraception.

FIONA: Sorry.

VARI: I've got mine off. Hurry up.

FIONA: Ready.

VARI: Right. I'm going to kiss your ear.

FIONA: Why?

VARI: That's what they do. Ready?

FIONA: Yes.

    (VARI *kisses* FIONA's *ear*.)

VARI: Right. That's that bit. Was it nice?

FIONA: Yes.

VARI: Now I'm going to kiss your mouth.

FIONA: No.

VARI: I've got to.

FIONA: I don't want you to.

VARI: It won't work if we don't do it properly.

FIONA: I don't like it.

VARI: All right, we'll skip the mouth bit. I'll just get on top of you.

FIONA: No.

VARI: Do you want to practise or not?

FIONA: All right.

VARI: Right. Try to just concentrate, will you. I mean you'd think we were doing something dirty.

FIONA: Sorry.

VARI: Right. (*Gets on top of* FIONA.) How's that? Am I heavy?

FIONA: No. Not really.

VARI: Do I feel nice?

FIONA: I suppose so.

VARI: Don't be so enthusiastic. I mean, I'm the one doing all the work.

FIONA: Sorry.

VARI: Right. I haven't got one so I'll just jig up and down a bit.

FIONA: Jigging.

VARI: What?

FIONA: Stop.

VARI: I don't want to.

FIONA: It's jigging, Vari. God'll see.

VARI: There's no God.

FIONA: It feels like jigging.

VARI: I told you there's no God.

FIONA: Aye. But what if there is?

VARI: What if?

FIONA: He'll look down and he'll see. Get off.

VARI: Not now.

FIONA: Get off.

VARI: Do you mean it?

FIONA: I mean it. I mean it. Get off.

VARI: I won't be your best friend any more.

FIONA: Sorry.

VARI: So am I.

FIONA: Will you be able to sleep?

VARI: I can always sleep.

FIONA: I really am awful sorry.

VARI: I'll just find someone else to practise with and you'll feel an awful idiot when you have to do it for real and you don't know how.

FIONA: Who will you find?

VARI: I'm not telling.

FIONA: Go on.

VARI: You're just like your Mum. My Mum says you can't hold back on a man. You won't keep a man either.

FIONA: My Mum says you've got to keep your kisses for the man you love and if you don't you're cheap and you didn't say there wasn't a devil and the devil gets you for jigging and that's a well-known fact and I don't care what you say we were jigging. I've got enough to contend with with bugs and bogies, never mind asking the devil to pay a visit too. Now you go home. I've a busy night ahead of me. I've 345 snakes in this bed and I've got to kill them all by morning and I haven't even reached the gun yet.

VARI: You're a prude, Fiona McBridie.

FIONA: Go away.

VARI: You just see if I care. (*Half goes.*) You're going to be half an orphan as good as and nobody'll like you any more. (*Blackout.*)

SCENE 2

1983
The beach. Bright sunlight.
MORAG *is on the rug.* FIONA *is drying herself.*

FIONA: Well?

MORAG: Is it your business?

FIONA: He was my Dad. You're my Mother.

MORAG: You've never asked before.

FIONA: I was very young when he went.

MORAG: That's about the sum of it.

FIONA: What?

MORAG: When your father left I was thirty-seven. I was very grateful to him that I wasn't forty. And that was my chief emotion. I knew he was going to go. All I prayed was that he'd not hang it out. It's a different thing trying to get another man at forty. At thirty-seven I even had another baby in me. Maybe. If some man hurried up.

FIONA: Why didn't you leave him?

MORAG: I loved him but if he went I didn't want to spend the rest of my life without a man. I like men. Not sex, you understand. That's dirty. Your father was like an elephant, if he got it once in ten years he could consider himself lucky. So he went. I could never see anything in it. With the telly now I can see I must have been wrong. I mean, there wouldn't be such a fuss if there was nothing in it.

FIONA: That's sad.

MORAG: Not in the least. You're thirty-two and you've not got a child. That's sad.

FIONA: I don't want one.

MORAG: Rubbish.

FIONA: I don't.

MORAG: Every woman wants a child.

FIONA: Not me.

MORAG: It's not as if your career's a success.

FIONA: It might be.

MORAG: I'm paying for this holiday.

FIONA: I only came to keep you company.

MORAG: I only came because you were looking so awful I thought you'd never get a man and that's all the thanks I get.

FIONA: I've got several men.

MORAG: Don't be dirty.

FIONA: Well, I have.

MORAG: Where are they then? I don't see them.

FIONA: They sure as hell aren't on the east coast of Scotland

having a quiet weekend with my Mother, being intruded
on by a best friend I haven't seen for seventeen years.

MORAG: Are you a lesbian? (*Pause.*) Don't look at me like that.
I'm only asking.

FIONA: I didn't even know you knew the word.

MORAG: Don't be silly. My own sister was one, of couse I know
the word.

FIONA: Who?

MORAG: Jane.

FIONA: Jane's married.

MORAG: Oh, aye, she did eventually but that was after.

FIONA: What?

MORAG: You haven't answered me.

FIONA: What?

MORAG: Are you a lesbian?

FIONA: I'm not going to answer you.

MORAG: I won't tell you about your Aunt Jane.

FIONA: Stuff you then.

MORAG: Don't talk to your Mother like that. It was a civilized
question. I expect a civilized answer.

FIONA: No, I'm not a lesbian, I just don't want a baby. Now,
what about Auntie Jane?

MORAG: I thought I'd have known about it. I mean you've
ruined my life with your other problems. I suppose you'd
have found some way to let me know about that. You know
what I'm talking about.
(*Pause.*)

FIONA: Tell me about Auntie Jane.

MORAG: Of course your Grandmother was appalled, sort of.

FIONA: Did she know?

MORAG: They did it under her roof. I always thought that was
most unwise. Your Grandmother threw them out, told
them to book into a hotel but she didn't want the sounds of
their pleasure coming through her bedroom ceiling. It was
bad enough with a man. It was an ATS sergeant. Your
Auntie Jane was between twenty and thirty and single in
the war years so she got conscripted. She'd have gone
anyway. She liked the uniform and she was awful patriotic.

23

That's why she emigrated to South Africa and not because of the scandal as some thought.

FIONA: What scandal?

MORAG: It was whispered up and down our street. The ATS sergeant was crop-haired. She had a low voice and a flat chest. She and Jane walked around arm in arm. The ATS sergeant was never out of uniform and Jane had always had a softness for frills. It was awful obvious. But that was when the bombs were falling on Clydebank and Glasgow. Your Grandmother relented. She thought her children should have their pleasure before a bomb got them. Whatever their pleasure might be. She didn't insist they left the house, just moved them to another bedroom so she didn't have to listen. Then they were next to me so that's how I knew for certain. I thought it might run in the family.

FIONA: What have we come here for?

MORAG: Well, that's a relief. I didn't quite know what kind of a face I was going to put on it if you were.

FIONA: Answer me.

MORAG: What, dear?

FIONA: Why have we come here?

MORAG: For a rest, dear.

1966
The beach.

VARI *runs down the rocks.*

VARI: Five numbers. One, two, three, four, five. One for kissing. Two for tongue in the mouth. Three for breast. Four for fingers. Five for your hand on him.

FIONA: What's after five?

(*Pause.*)

VARI: Six.

FIONA: What's number six?

VARI: It goes up to ten.

FIONA: What are the others?

VARI: Don't be dirty.

FIONA: You don't know.

VARI: How far have you gone?

FIONA: How far have you gone?

VARI: You first.

FIONA: No, you.

VARI: I asked you first.

FIONA: I asked you second.

VARI: Scaredy cat. I won't tell. I know. You're a whore. You've been to ten and back again. Only whores go to ten.

FIONA: Don't be silly.

VARI: Apart from mothers.

FIONA: What's number four?

VARI: His fingers up you. (*Silence*.) You're dirty.

FIONA: I didn't say I had, I just asked what it was. (*Silence*.) What do his fingers do up you?

VARI: Don't be daft.

FIONA: What do they do?

VARI: You know.

FIONA: What?

VARI: Wiggle about a bit.

FIONA: What does it feel like?

VARI: Haven't you ever . . . ? You know.

FIONA: What?

VARI: Done it to yourself.

FIONA: No. Should I? Is it nice?

VARI: It's all right.

FIONA: Is it nice when he does it?

VARI: Promise you won't tell.

FIONA: Promise.

VARI: Promise.

FIONA: Promise.

VARI: I've only done it once.

FIONA: When?

VARI: I'm telling you. Shut up. It was here. Up by the tunnel. Last Saturday. I was allowed out to eleven so . . .

FIONA: Ten o'clock, me.

VARI: Do you want to hear? We got down here and we were holding hands and that was a bit boring. I mean, he's not a great conversationalist.

25

FIONA: He's got lovely legs. And a black PVC raincoat.

VARI: We sat on that. It was warm last Saturday.

FIONA: Could you smell the shit from the sewers? I never think that's very romantic. What's wrong?

VARI: I'm just thinking I'm not going to tell you.

FIONA: I'm sorry.

VARI: You're always sticking your oar in.

FIONA: What did he stick?

(*They giggle and they giggle.*)

VARI: Anyway he kissed me. You know nice little nibbling ones not the great wet open-mouthed kind you get from some of them. Nice little nibbling things on the corner of my mouth and just down a bit. Then he put his tongue in my mouth and that got a bit boring so I took his hand and put it on my breast. My right breast, I think it was. He seemed to like that though he didn't do much. Then that got a bit boring so I put my hand on his thing. Don't look like that. There comes a time when you've got to, you know, take things into your own hands. So I did. I mean I'd never seen one except on statues. Anyway tit for tat. He was groping away so why shouldn't I? It was all hard. I suppose I should have expected that but it was an awful shock. I sort of rubbed away a bit. Then he did it. He got it out. He undid his trousers and out it came.

(*Pause.*)

FIONA: Well?

VARI: It was very big. How does that ever fit into you? It was all sort of stretched and a bit purple. Though I couldn't see very well. It seemed rude to stop and stare. I mean if you've got something like that I don't suppose you really want it looked at. He didn't. Cause he got on top of me. He pushed me over. He pulled up my skirt. He stuck his fingers up inside my pants and inside me. Then he rubbed a bit, you know, himself up and down on me. Then he sort of gasped and stopped. There was this great wet patch on my skirt when I got up. I told my Mum I'd dropped my ice-cream, you know, old-fashioned vanilla. Say something. Go on. You think I'm dirty.

26

FIONA: I don't.

VARI: You do.

FIONA: I was just wondering what number it was that you got to.

(EWAN, *long-legged and in black PVC, comes to the mouth of the tunnel.*)

VARI: Look.

FIONA: It's him.

VARI: Go on, he knows what to do. You try him.

FIONA: Me?

VARI: You like his legs.

FIONA: Another time.

VARI: Sure.

FIONA: He's waving to you.

VARI: There was this great lump of rock sticking in my back. I've got a bruise.

(VARI *goes off through the tunnel with* EWAN.)

1966

The bathroom.

MORAG: (*Calling from the bath*) Bring me my clothes and get yourself in here. I'll not call again.

FIONA: Here.

MORAG: Sit down, I want a word.

FIONA: (*Sits gingerly*) What?

MORAG: I'm forty-two years old.

FIONA: Did I not remember your birthday?

MORAG: Don't be daft. You don't look very comfortable.

FIONA: I'm all right. What do you want?

MORAG: Your Father left five years ago.

FIONA: I know that. (*She shifts, stands up, smooths her skirt at the back.*)

MORAG: Will you keep still, I'm trying to talk to you. Here, hold the towel, I'm getting out. (*She gets out. She's in a bathing suit. She drapes the towel.*) Here, look at me. I'm no half bad. I've always had a good figure, no one can deny me that. I've done my exercises through morning and night. My stomach's like a board. No baggy skin and I

27

never had any breasts so you won't see them sagging. If
you cut off my head you'd think I was nineteen. Pity about
my head. If I had money I'd go straight to a plastic
surgeon. A wee pull here, a stretch there. You've got St
Vitus's dance.

FIONA: You're a very attractive woman.

MORAG: Thank you, Fiona. Grooming. Always be smart. Even
if you're poor your clothes can be well brushed. You've not
been still since you came in here.

FIONA: Sorry.

MORAG: We've always had a good relationship, you and me.
Well? We have, haven't we?

FIONA: Yes.

MORAG: So. As I say, your Father left five years ago.

FIONA: Yes.

MORAG: Oh, Fiona, I've found a man. I'm in love. I never
really thought it would happen to me. I say I found him.
He really found me. I feel seventeen. I'm happy. I'm going
to ask him to the house and I wanted very humbly to ask
your permission. I want him to come to dinner and I
wanted you to meet him. What do you say?

FIONA: I've run out of sanitary towels.

MORAG: Pardon?

FIONA: I'm on the last one in the house and that's nearly
through. I'm going to get blood on my skirt.

MORAG: Go and buy some.

FIONA: You didn't order them from the Co-op.

MORAG: I forgot.

FIONA: You always order them with the messages.

MORAG: My mind wasn't on it. Can he come to dinner?

FIONA: What am I going to do?

MORAG: Put your coat on. Get some at the corner shop.

FIONA: No.

MORAG: Don't be daft. You can't not have sanitary towels.
That's dirty.

FIONA: Have you slept with him?

MORAG: There's money in my purse.

FIONA: I can't.

MORAG: Don't be stupid.

FIONA: There's a man in the corner shop.

MORAG: Men know women have periods.

FIONA: But he'll know it's actually coming out of me now. I'll be standing there bleeding in his shop and he'll know.

MORAG: Wait for the woman to come out from the back.

FIONA: You go.

MORAG: I will not.

FIONA: You're the one who forgot.

MORAG: You're the one who's bleeding.

FIONA: But I'm not a woman.

MORAG: Get the money from my purse and get along to that shop before you spoil your nice clothes.

FIONA: No.

MORAG: It'll be closed soon and then where'll you be?

FIONA: Bloody.

MORAG: You watch your tongue.

FIONA: I'm not going. You're my Mother. You're supposed to take care of me.

MORAG: You'll feel the back of my hand.

FIONA: I won't go. You forgot. You forgot.

MORAG: (*Dressing*) I saw you when you were born. Two hours I was in labour with you and you ripped me right up to my bum. You came out from between my legs and your eyes were open. You knew exactly what you'd done. The midwife held you up. You looked right at me. You didn't cry. No, madam. Not you. You gave me look for look. I didn't like you then and I don't like you now. Do you hear me, Fiona? Are you listening, Fiona? I don't like you. Nasty little black thing you were. You had hair to your shoulders and two front teeth. You wouldn't suck. I tried to feed you. I did everything that was proper. You'd take nothing from me. Your father took you. He dandled you and petted you. You had eyes for him all right. Well, he's not here now. You won't find him down at the corner s⸢ buying your sanitary towels. I took care of you. I clot⸢ you and washed you and you had your fair share of cuddles. Sometimes I even quite liked you. Thou⸢

gone your own way. You smoke, don't you? Don't you look at me like that. You walk back from that school every day, save the bus money for cigarettes. I know you do. I've seen you. I've not said. I've not said all I know about you. You sat on your father's knee, you clapped his head, you could get anything you wanted. You thought you could. You thought you could. You're still just a wee girl. Hanging round the prom on a Sunday teatime. I've seen you. Hanging round the boys. I've seen you, butter wouldn't melt in your mouth with your Sunday morning piety fresh on you and a smell of smoke on your breath. I've seen you looking at them. Sleekit smile on your face. You know it all. Well, do you, my girl? Do you know it all? You live in my house and in my house you do as I say, and if anything happens to you with your sly ways you'll not stay in my house. You'll be out the door and you'll not come back. What you ask for you get. Now go and buy your sanitary towels. (*Silence*.) I'm sorry. I love you. I'll always love you. I'm just out of the bath, Fiona. Are you asking me to catch my death?

FIONA: You've gone to bed with him.

MORAG: I'll not have you spreading blood on my furniture.

FIONA: You've let him touch you.

MORAG: Get the sanitary towels.

FIONA: It's a sin what you've done.

MORAG: Get to that shop.

FIONA: You're a sinner.

MORAG: Get.

FIONA: You're a whore.

(MORAG *hits* FIONA *hard*. MORAG *goes to the towel. She picks up a coat and goes down the tunnel*.)

1966
The beach.

VARI: (*Popping up*) Why did you not just go?

FIONA: It's dark.

VARI: So what?

FIONA: I'm scared of the dark.

30

VARI: If she gets a cold where'll you be?

FIONA: I don't care.

VARI: She wants to go away.

FIONA: Who?

VARI: Auntie Morag.

FIONA: Why?

VARI: Her man's got a job abroad. He's in oil. He's got to go to some Arab country or other. He wants her to go with him and she wants to go.

FIONA: She does not.

VARI: She does so.

FIONA: What about me?

VARI: You're not liable to get to university via the Trucial States so she asked my Mum if you could live with us, as a paying guest, seeing as we're friends.

FIONA: I don't want to live with you.

VARI: Why not?

FIONA: I want to live in my own house with my own mother. She can't go pissing off. She's responsible for me. She loves me.

VARI: She loves her man.

FIONA: When did she talk to your Mum?

VARI: The day before yesterday.

FIONA: Why didn't she tell me first?

VARI: She guessed how well you'd take it.

FIONA: I'll live with my Dad. He loves me.

VARI: Your Dad's got three wee kids of his own.

FIONA: I'm his own.

VARI: It's not an option.

FIONA: My Dad loves me.

VARI: Your Mum's checked it out. He doesn't want you. He said you could go for the odd weekend. You're not that easy to get on with. Adolescents never are.

FIONA: Where are the Trucial States?

VARI: On the Persian Gulf.

FIONA: There's oil here.

VARI: It's hotter over there and you don't have to live in the middle of the sea.

FIONA: She's a whore.

VARI: That's what my Mum says. My Mum says that them that come to it late are insatiable.

FIONA: It's my Dad's bed.

VARI: She doesn't want to live on her own for the rest of her life. My Mum's jealous. I don't think sex with my Dad's a party.

FIONA: I'm not going to let her go.

VARI: You can't stop her.

FIONA: I can.

VARI: How?

FIONA: I'll stop her.

1983
The beach.

MORAG: Oh, my God, would you look at that?

FIONA: It's a jellyfish.

VARI: Oh, God.

FIONA: It's not doing you any harm.

MORAG: I'll be the judge of that.

VARI: It's oozing, Auntie Morag.

MORAG: Get rid of it.

FIONA: What for?

VARI: It's obscene.

MORAG: I'm not sitting on the same beach as that.

FIONA: Oh, for goodness' sake.

VARI: It's all jelly.

MORAG: You. You wouldn't even kill a wasp. What are you doing?

(FIONA *has taken the sandwich container.*)

FIONA: Getting rid of it.

MORAG: You're not using that.

FIONA: You do it.

MORAG: That's a good sandwich box. I've used that year in, year out.

FIONA: It'll wash.

MORAG: Don't be so damned silly. I couldn't eat out of that again. It's sullied.

VARI: I stepped on a slug once, in the dark with my bare foot.

MORAG: When Fiona was a wee girl, she dived on top of a jellyfish in this very water. You'd think she'd show some sensitivity about my sandwich box.

FIONA: It's still alive.

MORAG: Spread its jelly all over her. Arms, legs, chest and face. Bright red she went and burning with fever. What are you doing?

FIONA: Putting it in the pool.

VARI: Oh, God, Fiona.

FIONA: The tide'll take it away.

MORAG: You might at least do the decent thing and stick it in a litter bin.

FIONA: I'm not killing it.

MORAG: Oh, for goodness' sake. Give it here. Give it to me.

FIONA: I will not.

MORAG: That's my box. Give it to me.

(FIONA *gives up the box.*)

I should think so. (MORAG *marches off to find a litter bin.*)

Fuss about a damn jellyfish.

VARI: Slugs, worms and jellyfish. I hate them.

(*Blackout.*)

ACT TWO

SCENE I

1966
The beach. The sun is shining.
EWAN *comes in from the sea. He settles on the hot rock.* FIONA
*comes on to the rocks through the tunnel. She's in her bikini. She
sees* EWAN. *She creeps to the pool and gathers water in her hands.
She moves over to* EWAN *and drops the water on him.*

EWAN: (*Screams*) Fucking cunt.
> (FIONA *moves away from him and sits staring out to sea.*
> EWAN *dries himself meticulously.*)
> Jesus Christ, woman. What do you expect, creeping up on
> a man like that? Took my breath away. I mean, Jesus,
> Fiona. That water's freezing. It's not the bloody
> Mediterranean. What the hell do you have to play bloody
> stupid games for? I mean, shit, Fiona. Come on. What's a
> man supposed to do? I mean, shit, Fiona. Shit. (*Pause.*)
> Come here. Look at the bloody face on it. Come here. I
> forgive you. Come on, I'll give you a cuddle. Bloody hell,
> woman. Bloody listen, will you. Move your backside over
> here. I've said I forgive you. Jesus Christ, what do you
> fucking well want? Dear God, woman, it's not as if I
> sodding well hit you. I mean, if I'd hit you you'd have
> something to bloody girn about. Don't be bloody
> ridiculous. (*Pause.*) You want me to say sorry to you. You
> sodding well do. You do. I sodding well won't. You've not
> a pissing hope. Shit. (*Pause.*) I'm fucking sorry. There. Is
> that bloody better?
> (FIONA *moves over to him.*)
> Bloody smile then.
FIONA: My Mum's going with a man.
EWAN: She's pretty, your Mum. I could fancy her.
FIONA: They sleep together in our house.
EWAN: Where do you expect them to go?
FIONA: It's disgusting.

34

EWAN: She's not that old, your Mum. Women probably need it
    as well as men. Your Dad left a long time ago.

FIONA: Shut up.

EWAN: It'd do you good.

FIONA: I'm not sixteen.

EWAN: What about it though?

FIONA: What?

EWAN: I could come to your house when your Mum's at work.

FIONA: My bedroom's at the front.

EWAN: That's nice for you. You'll have a sea view.

FIONA: Everyone'll see if I close the curtains during the day.

EWAN: Is that what's stopping you?

FIONA: They'll see you coming in, someone will even if you go
    round the back and if I close the curtains they'll know
    exactly what we're doing. The boy across the road hangs his
    penis out his upstairs window in his bare scuddy. The
    woman next door warned my Mum so that I wouldn't look
    but he only does it for me so it seems awful rude not to.
    He's always looking out for me so he can do it. He'd tell.
    The woman next door's got the police to him three times.
    She says she's got an interest in my welfare and he's a traffic
    hazard. He'd tell to get his own back. He thinks it's my
    fault he does it. You know, for being there. He was born in
    his house and we moved into ours and my bedroom's really
    the dining room so I shouldn't be there anyway. That's what
    he thinks. I'm always getting flashed at.

EWAN: Want a look?

FIONA: Don't be daft.

EWAN: You're very pretty.

FIONA: Thanks.

EWAN: Give us a kiss.

    (MORAG *is on the prom.* FIONA *and* EWAN *are necking on the*
    rocks.)

MORAG: Fiona. Come here. Come here.

FIONA: Oh, Christ.

EWAN: Leave this to me. Stay there.

FIONA: I'll have to come.

EWAN: I'll deal with it.

FIONA: All right but I'm coming too.

MORAG: Move yourself, Fiona.

(*They join* MORAG *above.*)

What do you think you're doing, the pair of you? You're in public.

EWAN: I must apologize, Mrs McBridie, it was entirely my fault.

MORAG: You were both getting your lips wet.

EWAN: At my behest.

MORAG: Indeed. And who are you?

EWAN: Ewan Campbell. I live up the Crescent.

MORAG: Do you?

EWAN: I do.

MORAG: You'll be the one at the bus stop in the uniform of the Academy.

EWAN: I've often admired your roses.

MORAG: Och, away with you. I know fine what you're trying to do. You won't get round me.

EWAN: Will you accept my apologies for kissing your daughter in public?

MORAG: You were half-way down her throat. If that was kissing times have changed.

EWAN: You've changed with them.

MORAG: Have I?

EWAN: May I take your daughter to the cinema?

MORAG: I said she wasn't to go out with a boy till she was sixteen.

FIONA: Please, Mum.

MORAG: You'll sit in the chummies and smooch all the way through the film.

EWAN: We'll endeavour to give you a good account of the story afterwards.

MORAG: I'll expect you to the house for tea before you go. Don't let me down again, the pair of you. There's plenty of time for that sort of thing when you're older.

FIONA: Your age.

MORAG: Mind your mouth.

EWAN: I'll be seeing you on Saturday then?

FIONA: Yes.

EWAN: Goodbye, Mrs McBridie.

MORAG: Aye.

(EWAN *goes out through the tunnel*.)

I want to talk to you.

FIONA: You were flirting with him.

MORAG: I'd be trying to get off with him right enough.

FIONA: I didn't want him to come to the house.

MORAG: I'm sorry. I thought he was your friend.

FIONA: You can have your man there and we'll be a cosy wee foursome. You can have one on either side and show off your winsome ways. Flutter your eyelashes.

MORAG: You've a cheap tongue.

FIONA: You wanted me.

MORAG: Yes.

FIONA: Is this it?

MORAG: What?

FIONA: You're going away. (*Pause*.) Why didn't you tell me?

MORAG: I couldn't.

FIONA: You're a whore and you're not even brave.

MORAG: Don't speak to me like that.

FIONA: Why didn't you tell me?

MORAG: I want to sell the house and go with him.

FIONA: I won't let you.

MORAG: In two years you'll be at university. I don't want to spend the rest of my life on my own.

FIONA: I might want to go to university here.

MORAG: You'll not want to stay with me.

FIONA: You're supposed to take care of me.

MORAG: If I could take you with me I would.

FIONA: Would you?

MORAG: I love you very much.

FIONA: You don't love me. Love. You love yourself. You love your reflection in a man's eyes. The first man that comes along you abandon me. Fuck you, Mother.

MORAG: Fiona.

FIONA: I don't want him in the house. (*She runs down to the beach*.)

1966
The beach.

VARI: What are you going to do? Have you decided?

FIONA: Know any good jokes?

VARI: What?

FIONA: I could do with a laugh.

VARI: What are you going to do?

FIONA: Right, I'll tell you one.

VARI: Is it dirty?

FIONA: Maybe.

VARI: Go on.

FIONA: I'm going to get pregnant.

VARI: You are not.

FIONA: I am so.

VARI: You can't.

FIONA: Wait and see.

VARI: Is that the joke?

FIONA: It'll stop her.

VARI: How will it?

FIONA: She can't go and leave me with a baby. I'm fifteen. What would people say? She'd care about that though she doesn't give a shit about me.

VARI: You'll wreck your life.

FIONA: No, I won't.

VARI: Who's going to do it?

FIONA: Ewan Campbell. Do you mind?

VARI: Does he? Do you fancy him?

FIONA: He's all right.

VARI: Why don't you come and stay with us?

FIONA: Your Mum's a bitch.

VARI: She's two-faced. She'd only be nasty behind your back. You can't sleep with someone you just think's all right.

FIONA: I thought you'd think it was a good idea.

VARI: It's a terrible idea.

FIONA: You've gone with him.

VARI: I'm a virgin and that's the way I'm going to stay till I get married which I'll do when I'm twenty-six, and have three very quick children and be back to work 'cause I'm not

going to be a skivvy like my Mum. My man'll have enough
money to buy a woman to do for me and private nurseries.

FIONA: What's the point in having them then?

VARI: You've got to have babies.

FIONA: Right.

VARI: Not when you're fifteen.

FIONA: Watch me. I'll be here on Saturday night after the film.
It's the right time in my menstrual cycle. I'll get pregnant.

VARI: You know an awful lot suddenly.

FIONA: I've been to the library.

VARI: You've not to do it.

FIONA: She'll bloody stay. I won't live on my own. She'll
bloody stay.

1983
The beach.

MORAG: (*From above*) I've brought ice-cream cones. You can't
have a holiday without ice-cream cones. Where are your
three lovely children?

VARI: My Mum takes them for a morning sometimes.

MORAG: That'll give you a wee break. She'll be very proud of
you, your Mum.

VARI: Sorry?

MORAG: Your big house and your fine doctor husband.

VARI: She thinks I'm mad.

MORAG: Why is that, dear?

VARI: I went in for Shona, my third. I told her. She didn't
speak to me for six months. Said if I wanted to ruin my life
it was my affair.

MORAG: I see.

VARI: Look at me. I'm fat. I've seen you, Fiona. You can't keep
your eyes off my tummy. I strip myself at night. He's not
often there so no one sees. I look at myself in the mirror.
This is a mother's body. Where am I? Don't think I pity
myself. I wanted this from when I was wee. I'm feeling
puzzled. Where am I? My tits have got great blue veins
running across them. They look good when they're full of
milk but then it's mostly running down my front so the

effect's somewhat spoilt. When they're empty they're poor things. All the exercises in the world'll not save my stomach. The doctor's face when I'd had Moira. He pulled out a handful of skin. I said that'll go away won't it. He let it go. Splat. He shook his head. He looked awful sad. He probably knows Archie. Felt sorry he had to make love to a doughbag for the rest of his life. I mean, I could have an operation. Archie's said already about it. They take away all the stretched-out skin. You end up looking like a hot cross bun. They cut you from here to here and up. I'd rather buy a corset. I mean, God or no God, you're asking for it if you fiddle. I mean, I'm healthy. You can have it on the National Health, the operation. Archie wouldn't compromise his principles even for the sake of his own pleasure. There's always divorce.

MORAG: What God's intended God's appointed.

FIONA: Don't say that.

VARI: Listen, it's easier if he's not there. I can handle the children. I eat what they eat. We get on fine. When he's in he enquires politely about the mess, makes requests about the level of the noise and I have to cook him dinner. It's not his fault. He's got his work. He likes a cooked breakfast too. Archie's very good to me. He lets the babies sleep in the bed with me and he goes to another room. We're lucky we have a good big house. That way he gets his sleep and I only have to turn over when they wake in the night. Of course we don't make love but I wake up covered in milk and piss, I can do without sperm as well. I beg your pardon, Auntie Morag.

FIONA: Do you miss sex?

VARI: I've read every book in existence on the female orgasm. I've never had one.

MORAG: Still. We'll get into heaven. (*Pause.*) You're very quiet, Fiona. (*Pause.*) Though you're my own daughter and I love you, I have to say it. You were always common.

(MORAG *throws a travelling rug round her shoulders and slowly leaves.* VARI *and* FIONA *sit in the gloaming of evening.*)

1966
The beach.
EWAN *comes in through the tunnel.*
EWAN: Where are you? Stop playing bloody silly games.
FIONA: I'm here.
>   (VARI *moves into the shadows.*)
EWAN: Where did you get the towel?
FIONA: I left it here this afternoon.
EWAN: It'll be damp.
FIONA: The rocks keep their heat.
EWAN: What number do you go to?
FIONA: I go up to ten and back again.
EWAN: Christ.
FIONA: It's your lucky night.
EWAN: Are you serious?
FIONA: Yes.
EWAN: I haven't got a thing.
FIONA: What?
EWAN: French letter.
FIONA: Never mind.
EWAN: Are you kidding me?
FIONA: No.
EWAN: You're not one of them?
FIONA: What?
EWAN: They're low.
FIONA: Who?
EWAN: PTs.
FIONA: No.
EWAN: You're not a virgin then?
FIONA: Do you want to do it?
EWAN: I think so.
FIONA: Make up your mind.
EWAN: I'm surprised.
FIONA: Have you done it before?
EWAN: I've gone quite far.
FIONA: Right then.
EWAN: What?
FIONA: Let's start.

EWAN: Are you sure it's safe?

FIONA: Do you want to or not?

EWAN: Are you going to take your clothes off?

FIONA: It's not that warm.

EWAN: You don't sound very excited.

FIONA: Neither do you.

EWAN: It takes a bit of getting used to.

FIONA: You do fancy me?

EWAN: Yes. Yes, of course I do.

FIONA: Do you think I'm cheap for wanting to do it?

EWAN: I respect you.

FIONA: Right then. We could kiss first.

EWAN: Yes, of course.

> (VARI *creeps up as they kiss.*)

VARI: That doesn't look very exciting.

FIONA: It's not.

VARI: Better do something.

FIONA: What?

VARI: Bite his ear.

FIONA: That's not very original.

VARI: Just do it.

> (FIONA *bites* EWAN's *ear.*)
>
> His hand moved. Stick your tongue in.

FIONA: Where?

VARI: His ear, stupid. Go on.

> (FIONA *does as she's told.*)
>
> Has he got a hard-on?

FIONA: I don't know.

VARI: Find out.

FIONA: How?

VARI: Do you want me to do it for you?

FIONA: No.

VARI: Stick your hand on it.

> (FIONA *does.*)
>
> Don't be so rough. Is it hard?

FIONA: I think so.

VARI: Lie down.

FIONA: Where?

VARI: On your back.

FIONA: I haven't any knickers on. Do you think he'll get a fright?

VARI: How do I know?

FIONA: You practically did it with him.

VARI: What did you take your knickers off for?

FIONA: I thought they'd get in the way.

VARI: He's puffing a bit. His hand's moved right up your leg.

FIONA: This is quite exciting.

VARI: Lie down quick.

(FIONA *moves away from* EWAN *and lies on the towel.*)

FIONA: He hasn't touched my tit yet. He should, shouldn't he?

VARI: It's not compulsory.

FIONA: I thought you had to.

VARI: Considering what you're offering a tit's a bit tame.

(EWAN *moves on top of* FIONA.)

FIONA: Is this it?

VARI: Has he got it out?

FIONA: I don't know.

VARI: You must know.

FIONA: What if he comes before it's in?

VARI: I don't know. Do you like it?

FIONA: Yes. Ouch.

VARI: What?

FIONA: It's in.

VARI: You're dirty.

FIONA: You can go.

(VARI *goes.*)

EWAN: You were a virgin.

FIONA: So were you.

EWAN: You must love me an awful lot.

FIONA: Do you want to do it again?

EWAN: Why?

FIONA: Didn't you like it?

EWAN: Yes, but . . .

FIONA: What?

EWAN: Did you?

FIONA: Yes. Well. Very nearly.

EWAN: You're not supposed to, are you?

FIONA: Why not?

EWAN: You're female. Whores enjoy it.

FIONA: Are you saying I'm a whore?

EWAN: I don't know, do I?

FIONA: I was a virgin.

EWAN: Do you love me?

FIONA: No, I don't.

EWAN: What did you do it for then?

FIONA: You're not to tell anyone.

EWAN: I won't.

FIONA: If I hear you've told; if I hear a word about this night on the beach, I'll say you couldn't do it.

EWAN: I thought it would be different. (*Pause.*) Are you angry with me?

FIONA: You're the only other one here.

EWAN: What did you do it for?

FIONA: You did it too.

EWAN: Will I see you again?

FIONA: I'll be getting the bus on Monday morning.

EWAN: I mean see you.

FIONA: I know fine what you mean.

EWAN: Well?

FIONA: Go home, Ewan.

EWAN: I promised your Mum I'd see you safe to your front door.

FIONA: What could happen to me?

EWAN: You know.

FIONA: Tell me.

EWAN: What's up with you?

FIONA: Tell me.

EWAN: Rape. Fiona. I could give you a cuddle.

FIONA: Och, Ewan, it'll not fix itself. Go away and leave me alone.

EWAN: Come here.

FIONA: Just go away, will you. Please.

EWAN: I'll see you on Monday morning.

FIONA: I do like you.

(EWAN *goes through the tunnel.*)

VARI: So. Now we wait.

FIONA: Och, shut up.

(VARI *goes, singing 'Bye, Bye, Blackbird'.* FIONA *stays on the beach and joins in for two or three verses.*)

All right. I've made a mistake. I won't get pregnant. I won't get pregnant. I bet I won't. I bet I won't. Virgins don't very often get pregnant first off. It'll be tonight. That'll be the end of it and I won't speak to him again. He can be at the bus stop all he likes, I won't so much as look at him. Stuck-up pig. Who does he think he is, with his great long legs and his manners? Stuff his manners. Stuff him. I mean, it takes two. He didn't have to. He could have said no. Stupid black PVC raincoat. He thinks he's great. He's not, he's not. I'll swim in the sea. I'll wash him all off me. He'll be nowhere. I'll wash him all out of me. He won't exist. He won't be in me. He'll be in his stupid piece of black plastic and nowhere else. I'll be clear. I'm so cold.

MORAG: Fiona. What are you doing?

FIONA: Nothing.

MORAG: Are you all right?

FIONA: I'm fine.

MORAG: Do you know what the time is?

FIONA: Late.

MORAG: You shouldn't be on the rocks at this hour. You should have come straight home after the pictures. I've sat up waiting.

FIONA: Come for a swim.

MORAG: What's the matter with you?

FIONA: I feel like a swim.

MORAG: It's the middle of the night.

FIONA: Best time.

MORAG: It's cold.

FIONA: Keep your clothes on.

MORAG: All right.

FIONA: You're kidding.

MORAG: In, under and out. Race you.

FIONA: You're kidding.

MORAG: Race you. Come on.

FIONA: You're mad. It's bloody freezing in there.

MORAG: It's your idea.

FIONA: You're on.

MORAG: On your marks, get set, go.

    (*They rush in.*)

    Oh, my God.

FIONA: Jesus Christ.

MORAG: Beat you.

FIONA: It's a draw.

MORAG: I got in first.

FIONA: I was under first.

MORAG: Last one out's a cissy.

FIONA: Ready, steady, go.

    (*They race out on to the rocks.*)

    Jesus.

MORAG: Come here and give me a cuddle.

    (*They put their arms round each other.*)

    What happened?

FIONA: When?

MORAG: You were upset.

FIONA: I'm bloody freezing.

MORAG: We'll have a mug of hot chocolate when we get in.

FIONA: Me for the bath first.

MORAG: Was it wandering hands?

FIONA: Yes.

MORAG: You just have to be firm.

FIONA: I was.

MORAG: That's all right, then.

FIONA: Mum . . .

MORAG: What?

FIONA: Race you to the house.

    (*Blackout.*)

SCENE 2

1983
The beach. The sun is shining.
FIONA *is sitting with a towel round her shoulders.* VARI *is on the travelling rug.*

VARI: Do you find it much changed?

FIONA: It's the same.

VARI: You're not looking. See round the corner. There's a nuclear power station.

FIONA: Where?

VARI: Breathe in. Go on. Through your nose. What do you smell?

FIONA: Air.

VARI: There you are, you see. No sewers. You can't smell the shit, can you?

FIONA: Where is it? This nuclear power station.

VARI: It's like a fairy palace when it's all lit up.

FIONA: You like it.

VARI: Away back there. The sun shines off the sea and the glass of the reactors. It's a jewel in the green trees.

FIONA: Don't be daft.

VARI: There's building dirt from the B reactor. That's begun now. Do you know what they're doing with the dirt? Do you?

FIONA: Tell me.

VARI: Land from the sea. They're reclaiming it. See, that's creative. That shows conscience. And the work isn't allowed to disturb the environment. On that site there's flowers and trees. That's considerate. They fixed the sewers.

FIONA: You live round the corner from that.

VARI: I'm not the only one.

FIONA: Come on.

VARI: Lots of people do.

FIONA: For Christ's sake.

47

VARI: It's clean. It's awful pretty. All those lights twinkling like stars in the black night.

FIONA: Waste.

VARI: My mother always said it doesn't matter what the house is like, it can be a midden as long as the bathroom's clean. Then you know the woman of the house hasn't been got by the Apathy. I mean this place. It was a shit bin. I've three children. Shit can kill. Dog shit. People shit. My children wouldn't have been allowed near this beach if the sewers hadn't been fixed. Because they might tire me out but I love them.

FIONA: It wasn't as bad as that.

VARI: Wasn't it?

FIONA: How many reactors are there going to be?

VARI: A, B and C. You haven't kids, what do you know? You were never a mother.

FIONA: What was I then?

VARI: Down the road the old coal-fired place belting its muck out. Remember? Wind off the sea, shit; wind from the West, smoke. It's shut down now. Breathing that stuff. You don't live here. I mean, having the baby, it was a hiccup for you. You dropped it, passed it on, gave it away. You know nothing. It had no effect on your life. You changed schools. You got to university. Look at you now. No responsibilities. What do you know? It was all taken care of for you.

FIONA: I was fifteen.

VARI: I'm thirty-two. Sometimes I feel fifty. You got away with it. Slender young thing. I hate you.

FIONA: If there's an accident with the reactors your kids will suffer.

VARI: See, you. You've changed. You've got thinner. Me, I'm always going to be lumpy. So I hate you. Your face is taut, you've got cheek-bones. You've got the make-up right in the corner of your eyes. That takes time. I haven't got time. You'll be a member of CND and some left-wing political group with militant affiliations and pacifist intent. You'll wear dungarees, speak harsh words of men and belong to a feminist

48

encounter group where you look up your genitals with a
mirror. I watch telly. Of course your blouses come from
market stalls ten a penny but your shoes cost a packet. I know
you. I've seen you on demonstrations on the telly. I haven't
got time. I keep my hair short for it's less bother that way. I
wear a pair of elastic panties from Marks and Spencer's to
keep my tummy in and to stop my bum from shoogling. I play
badminton once a week in the same church hall we had the
youth club in when we were young and I promise myself I'll
have a sauna in some health club and a weekend in London
when my youngest is weaned. If Archie says I can. For he's
got the money. I have acquired a major accomplishment.
Compromise. Listen. This is what I chose. I'm happy till you
march in with no bottom and a social conscience.

FIONA: I'm sorry.

VARI: What for? You can't help it any more than I can. But get
it right, Fiona, get it right. (VARI *wanders down and stands
looking out to sea.*)

1966

The beach.

FIONA: (*Very quickly*) Last week, I was on the bus, upstairs. I
was going to see Dorothy and this girl up the front, she
started having a fit or something. Must have been the heat.
There were lots of people there between her and me but
they, none of them . . . I went over to her and did what I
could. She was heavy. I'd heard about them biting through
their tongues. Epileptics. It wasn't pretty. Me and this
other bloke took her to the hospital. But I saw her first. He
wouldn't have done anything if I hadn't. I didn't get to see
Dorothy. Well? That's worth something, isn't it? God. Are
you listening? I'm not trying to bribe you. It's plain
economics. I mean, I've made a mistake. It was my fault
and I was wrong. I take it all on me. OK. Now if you let it
make me pregnant . . . God. Listen, will you. If I'm
pregnant it'll ruin four people's lives. Five. Right? My
Mum'll be disappointed and her man'll walk out on her.
That's two. Are you with me, God? I'll not be very happy.

My Mother'll hate me for the rest of my life for what I've done and that's not easy to live with. That's three. I'm still counting, God. Ewan'll be in for it. Well, he can't avoid it. I'm illegal and I've never been out with anybody else. Not that nobody fancied me. I wouldn't like you to think I was unpopular. Lots of people fancied me. My Mum said I had to wait till I was sixteen. Then she relented just when Ewan happened to be there. Poor old Ewan. That's four, God, that's four. Then there's the baby. If it's there and if I have it it's got no chance. It would be born in Scotland. Still there, are you? I hate Scotland. I mean, look at me. If I have an abortion the baby'll be dead so that'll be five anyway.

VARI: Who the hell are you talking to?

FIONA: 'scuse me. Cover your ears.

VARI: Eh?

FIONA: Do it. This is private. Thank you. Sorry, God. You'll see from the aforegoing that you really don't need another soul in the world through me. You could let my Mum have a miracle baby with her man. She's only forty-two. It's still possible and she'd be really chuffed if you would. So we'll regard that as settled, then. Thank you very much for your attention. You can deal with something else now. Amen.

VARI: There's no God.

FIONA: I know.

VARI: What are you doing then?

FIONA: You were listening.

VARI: What do you expect? How are you feeling?

FIONA: Fine, thanks. How are you?

VARI: You know what I mean.

FIONA: The fair on Saturday. Did you go? I stayed on the chairoplanes for half an hour. It cost me a fortune. I was sick when I got off.

VARI: What for?

FIONA: I thought I might shake it loose.

VARI: You think it's there then?

FIONA: I don't know.

VARI: When are you due?

FIONA: Next week.
VARI: I can't stand the suspense. It's making me itchy.
FIONA: Look. It's my Mum.
    (MORAG *is above*.)
VARI: So what?
FIONA: You're not to say anything.
MORAG: Dinner's ready.
FIONA: Can Vari come? Will there be enough food?
VARI: I've got my dinner waiting for me at home.
MORAG: My man'll be there.
FIONA: That'll be nice. You're coming.
VARI: Don't order me about.
FIONA: Please.
VARI: I'll have to phone my Mum.
    (*Blackout*.)

SCENE 3

1966
The beach.
FIONA *is alone on the beach in the sunshine*.

FIONA: Three old ladies with shopping bags. God. One blind
    woman to the hairdresser's. That was a hard one. It was
    right out of my way. How many stars do I get for that? I
    mean, do you deal in stars as well as black marks? God.
    Here's the biggie. I fixed it for my Mum to go with her
    man. I don't want to be left. You've got to realize I've
    made a big sacrifice. I've been completely unselfish. How
    many people can come here and say that to you, God? I've
    done something entirely for someone else. Are you
    impressed? Are you? I've fixed it for my Mum to go to the
    Trucial States with her man. His name's Robert, just so
    you know. I'm going to go to Vari's. You really should do
    something about her Mother. Talk about black marks. So
    it's fixed. Were you around when I did it? It was at the
    dinner table. He was there, Robert, and so was Vari. I said,
    'By the way. I think you two need to be alone together for

the start of your marriage. Why don't you take your
honeymoon on the Gulf? I'll be very happy to stay with
Vari and I hope you two'll be happy for you have my
blessing.' I did it just like that. Sort of formal and casual at
the same time. The right touch, I thought. Vari giggled.
My Mum. Did you see? My Mum lit up. I've never seen
her look like that. She's always had these graven lines from
her nose to her mouth. Way since I can remember. They
went. Daft, eh, God? Bet you weren't looking. I've never
seen anyone look happy like that. He, Robert, looked more
than a wee bit pleased too. I don't want her to go. I'll have
nobody it doesn't matter with. I won't have somebody of
my own. I'll have to write letters. I hate writing letters.
Still, I think it's worth it. Don't you, God? They say I can
go out for the school holidays. I'll like that fine. Listen to
me, God. You've not to let those little fish meet the seed.
Let them chase their own tails. Anything you like. Kill
them of. Don't let them make a baby. God. God. Are you
there? God. Come on. Och, damn you then.

(EWAN *comes down through the tunnel on to the rocks.*)

EWAN: Hello.

FIONA: Hello.

EWAN: How have you been?

FIONA: Fine.

EWAN: I've not seen you at the bus stop.

FIONA: I've been getting the 42.

EWAN: I see.

    (*Pause.*)

FIONA: How have you been?

EWAN: Very well, thank you.

FIONA: And your studies?

EWAN: Fine. What about you?

FIONA: Prime university material.

EWAN: That's good then.

FIONA: Yes. (*Pause.*) You don't have to be polite because we've
    fucked.

    (*Pause.*)

EWAN: I hear your Mother's going away.

FIONA: That's the idea.

EWAN: When?

FIONA: It'll be a couple of months yet. (*Pause.*) Did you know that the moment of conception can take place up to two days after a fuck? I mean, you don't just do it and boom you're pregnant. It can take up to two days of swimming. I wonder what I was doing when I conceived.

EWAN: I don't . . .

FIONA: I could have been having a piss at the time or playing netball. I've been playing a lot of netball and badminton and tennis. I've been swimming. Hockey's over but I've been playing volleyball. Two a side. It's a fast game. I've fallen over a lot. Look at this knee. It's had a terrible thumping. We won the school badminton tournament, me and my partner. We were rank outsiders. A hundred-to-one shot. I could have been playing badminton when I conceived. My O levels start next week.

EWAN: Are you pregnant by me?

FIONA: That was the idea.

EWAN: Why?

FIONA: I love you madly and I want to be your wife.

EWAN: Will you marry me?

FIONA: Very noble.

EWAN: Well?

FIONA: How old are you?

EWAN: Seventeen next month.

FIONA: I'm fifteen. I don't want to marry you. I don't want to marry anyone and I don't want to have a baby.

EWAN: Don't you like me?

FIONA: Not much. I'm sure you're a very nice person but you're not really my type.
(*Pause.*)

EWAN: You're being honourable.

FIONA: No.

EWAN: You couldn't have done it with me if you hadn't loved me.

FIONA: It was quite exciting.
(*Pause.*)

EWAN: What are we going to do?

FIONA: It's nothing to do with you.

EWAN: It's my child.

FIONA: You were the donor. That's all. You're not to tell anyone. I'm doing my O levels in peace.

EWAN: Will you get rid of it?

FIONA: Probably. Now go away.

(*He gets up to go.*)

Ewan. Do you love me?

EWAN: I could get used to the idea.

FIONA: If you didn't love me why did you do it? Promise you won't tell.

(EWAN *goes through the tunnel*.)

I wasn't christened. That's what's wrong, isn't it? I was a lost soul to begin with. I'll get christened if you'll take it away. Do me a favour, will you, God. It's not my fault I wasn't christened. I feel sick all the time and I've got to get through my O levels. Churches make me cry. I'll believe in you if you'll take this away. I don't like it at all.

(VARI *enters*.)

VARI: You're getting fat.

FIONA: I know.

VARI: You'll have to tell. Your Mum's going in a fortnight.

FIONA: She's sold the house.

VARI: You shouldn't have let her do that. What does it feel like?

FIONA: Heavy. I'm tired all the time.

VARI: Isn't it nice?

FIONA: No.

VARI: I think you're lucky. You'll never be alone again.

(MORAG *comes through the tunnel*.)

FIONA: Shut up. Jesus, that's stupid.

MORAG: I've bought so many things. Fiona, I bought you two dresses. I took a guess at the size. You're chubby these days but awful pretty. Take them back if you don't like them. Vari, I've bought you a jumper. You've a nice bust. It's a skinny rib. Here. It'll show you off. You mind with the boys now. Fiona, I've one for you too. You're getting a bust yourself. Think yourself lucky. I've done without all my life. That'll be your father's side of the family.

VARI: You shouldn't have bought anything for me. Auntie Morag.

MORAG: Don't you like it?

VARI: It's lovely. Thank you very much.

MORAG: Fiona?

FIONA: It's smashing.

MORAG: I wish you both health to wear them.

VARI: And happiness.

MORAG: You'll have that, all right. You're fair good girls.

FIONA: OK, God. I'm not going to tell her. This is what I've decided. You're to back me up now, you hear. I'll do it on my own. After she's gone. After the O levels, I'll go down to London and get an abortion and don't you come it. You've left me no choice. I mean, it wasn't much to ask. She'll leave me money. She's bound to. Vari and me'll say we're going to visit friends. Kate Alex, her that had the restaurant, she moved to London. She'll back us. All you've got to do. Are you listening? Don't let me down this time. All you've got to do is not let me show till after she's gone and the O levels are past. I mean, chubby's all right but I don't want any bumps. Now listen to me. You've done nothing I've asked so far. Don't go trying anything off your own bat. I've taken the initiative. No bumps. Right? Right, God? Right?

MORAG: Fiona.

FIONA: What?

(*Silence.* FIONA *and* MORAG *looks at each other.*)

Hey, God.

(*Silence.*)

1966
The beach.

EWAN *is at the tunnel entrance.* FIONA *walks over to him.*

FIONA: You're a wee shit, aren't you?

EWAN: I did it for the best.

FIONA: What best? Who's best? What were you? Playing the
fucking hero. Is that it?

EWAN: I hardly think . . .

FIONA: No, you don't, do you? You don't think. What did you
think was gonnie happen? Come on. I'm interested. What
did you think you'd accomplish with your blabbing mouth?
What did you think? What did you think? I'm fucking
fascinated to know.

EWAN: I thought . . .

FIONA: I can see you, standing there with your head bowed.
Did you bow your wee head, Ewan, in all humility: Did
you duck your wee fat bonce? Were your big bony knees
shaking? Were you humble? 'I'm awfully sorry, Mrs
McBridie, but your dear sweet daughter Fiona, of whom
I'm awfully fond, I hope you'll forgive me but I stuck one
up her and now she's in the family way.' Is that your style,
Ewan? Is it? Did it go like that? Did I get it right? Answer
me.

EWAN: I think . . .

FIONA: No, not you. Did you come the big man? Did you stand
there tall, your proud head held high? Up on your high
arse. 'I've done wrong, Mrs McBridie. Fiona's pregnant. I
have no apologies to make. I'm prepared to marry her.'
Was that it, Ewan? Or did you tell her her daughter's a
whore? Did you sit her down with a nice wee drink? Did
you bring her a bunch of flowers? Did you walk her round
the garden? How did you tell her? Come on. Come on.
Answer me. Cunt.

(EWAN *hits* FIONA. *Silence.*)

That's a mighty answer. There's a big man. Potent and
virile. He can fuck a bint and he can swing his fists too.

EWAN: It wasn't easy.

FIONA: No.

EWAN: I felt I had to.

FIONA: Yes.

EWAN: You couldn't go on alone.

FIONA: What do you think I'm going to be now? I was getting
on fine with my mother and she liked me. We were turning

into good companions. What do you think you've done to
that?

EWAN: You're pregnant.

FIONA: Congratulations.

EWAN: Fiona.

FIONA: Och, well.

EWAN: I felt I had to.

FIONA: Go away.

EWAN: I . . .

FIONA: Go away.

(EWAN *goes out.* FIONA *sits on the towel.*)

1983

The beach.

MORAG: We've had beautiful weather. We've been that lucky
with the weather. Of course, we were always tanned when
we lived here. In the summer months. Now they're saying
it's not good for you, the sun. I can't see that that's right. I
mean too much of anything . . . Look at orange juice and
that man. Or was it carrots that killed him? But that was
plain silly. Sun. In this country. How can you get too
much? And they made that pool with their own hands.
Men. They brought their wee tools and they chiselled it out
in the hot days. Drinking their beer and telling their dirty
jokes. Well, they would, wouldn't they? Men do. They
built it to save their feet on the hot rocks. Great soft things.
Fancy going to all that trouble to save a 15-yard walk. They
never brought their wives. Of course, that was when I was
wee. When I think of it now, I think they must have been
the unemployed. They were here an awful lot. Nice men
they were too. They got raucous as the day went on with
the beer and then I wasn't allowed near the beach. The
storms there were. Summer and winter. You'd see the
spray coming right up over the roofs of the houses. I used
to stand in the mouth of the tunnel. I used to dare the
waves to come and get me. I'd run forward and I'd run
back. My Mum'd leather me for being wet when I got in.
It was worth it. Once I asked her for a raincoat. A special

present for my birthday. A real waterproof. I wanted it to keep me dry from the spray. She bought it for me. It was a real one. Kept me snug and dry. When I got in my Mum belted me across the face. She had a hard hand. Then she chased me round the house with the bread knife. For getting the raincoat wet. She was angry. I feel so disappointed.

FIONA: We could have gone to the Lakes for Christ's sake.

MORAG: I'll love you whatever you do. You know that. I've loved you through it all.

FIONA: Don't be stupid.

MORAG: You're my daughter.

FIONA: If I tortured, if I murdered, you'd love me then?

MORAG: You're my flesh and blood.

FIONA: It means nothing. (*She clicks her fingers.*) It means *that*. It's an insult, Mother.

MORAG: I stood by you.

FIONA: Is that why we've come here?

MORAG: I wanted to talk. I couldn't talk to you. You're a queer lass but I love you.

FIONA: Did it ever occur to you, you had a choice?

MORAG: What?

FIONA: You had a choice. Did you know that? Did you know you had a choice?

MORAG: Suppose I did?

FIONA: Oh, Jesus.

MORAG: Further and further away from me. The years pass. Each day. Vegetarian food. Symphonies. You put up barriers and I'm . . . We never had a symphony in the house. There was no need. I mean, I had other things . . . Time was, I'd go out, I'd buy you something. Impulse. I'd be in a shop. Some wee thing. You'd like it. I'd know you'd like it. Now. I wanted to talk to you. Books. I don't like Dickens. I never did. I like Georgette Heyer and I like the television. I'm very fond of the television. Your flat. You've not got an ashtray in your flat. Not a single one.

FIONA: I don't smoke.

MORAG: Of course you don't smoke. Live and let live. I've

always said that. I hold to that. You have men and I say nothing though I'd like it if you'd talk to me. For years I held down a good job.

FIONA: I know you did.

MORAG: I'm not a stupid woman.

FIONA: I never said . . .

MORAG: Choice, choice, choice. Yes, yes. I knew there was a choice. Let me find the right word. I like to have the right word. The exact right word. Culpable. You and me. See now. I know you're not all to blame. I'm culpable. Not the going away.

FIONA: What then?

MORAG: I mean, I met a man and I loved him. I met a man and I was glad he wanted me. Do you see? I wanted to go away with him. So what's more natural than that? Come on.

FIONA: I told you to . . .

MORAG: See me now. Look. I knew what I'd become. I made a break for something. OK. When he came to me, Ewan. When he came to me and told me.

FIONA: Mum, this is . . .

MORAG: You listen. 'Mrs McBridie, Fiona's going to have a child. It's my child. I'm sorry, Mrs McBridie.' Oh, he was polite. I liked him. Poor wee fella. I liked him fine.

FIONA: He was . . .

MORAG: Now listen to me. I knew I had a choice. Listen. My daughter had not come to me. Do you understand that? My daughter was not asking for my help. I could see her point. Listen. I had a choice. What if I left her enough money and I went away? Nothing mentioned between us. I knew you'd not have that child. Then you might say we'd survive, you and me. Out of the question. Fifteen and pregnant. Of course I couldn't let you alone. So. You told Ewan. So. Here we both are. Here we are. (*Pause*.) I expect you'd like an ice-cream cone. I'll walk up the prom a bit. My last walk of this holiday. I don't expect you ever will talk to me. Would you like a double 99 with raspberry sauce? That's what I'm having. My own wee treat. Will you join me? You've got to do something daft on a last day.

FIONA: That would be lovely.

MORAG: Don't if you'd rather not.

FIONA: Bunny rabbit's ears. A double 99.

MORAG: You'll join me then?

FIONA: Yes.

MORAG: After all, it's not meat.

FIONA: I'll join you.

MORAG: That's good then. That's very good.

> (*She goes off up the tunnel.* VARI's *voice comes from beside the swimming pool.*)

VARI: Your Mother's alive. They all are, that generation. My Mother's the same. She's an old cow but she's zinging with it. Life. Me, sometimes I get this awful dizzy feeling. I'm standing there. I'm doing something. I don't know what day of the week it is. I panic. I mean, I really don't know. I hang on to myself. If I don't I'll fall down. I put my arms round myself and hug tight. I hug very tight. I look out the window to see what the weather's like. See, I don't know where I am in the year. And I'm dizzy. I lean my back to the sink. I check the big tree outside the window. If it's got leaves. I look down at my clothes. What's the month? What month is it? What year is it? How many children have I got? Am I pregnant now? Have I just given birth? I don't know. I don't know. And then it comes to me. It's Wednesday. It's October. It's Sunday. It's April. It's all the same and I turn back to the sink. I wash the nappies by hand. I've got a washing machine, don't you worry. One of the ones that does it all. You know, dries as well. I've a dish-washer too. I wash the nappies by hand. They're cleaner that way. Not that I care. I don't care, but you have to have something to talk about at mothers' mornings. Do something queer. Marks you out.

FIONA: My Mother cares passionately about everything. Life and a ham sandwich. It all has the same importance. Not a touch of the Apathy. God? Do you still live here or have you moved on? Hung up your omniscience and retired the Recording Angel? Would it be too much to ask, I'd liked to be let alone?

> (MORAG *comes through the tunnel with the ice-creams.*)

MORAG: Bunny rabbit's ears. The raspberry sauce is running down my hands. Here, take it quick, Fiona. I'd have brought you one, Vari, if I'd known. Here, have one of my ears.

VARI: Thank you, Auntie Morag.

MORAG: I've some whisky in my bag. Reach me it over. Our last day. You'll drink with us, the Parting Glass. Eat your ice-cream, Fiona. A wee bit of what you fancy. (*She one-handedly arranges glasses and begins to unscrew the bottle as the lights fade down.*)

WHEN WE WERE WOMEN

CHARACTERS

MAGGIE	A woman of forty-five
ISLA	Her daughter
ALEC	Isla's father
MACKENZIE	A Chief Petty Officer in the Royal Navy
CATH	A woman

The action takes place in Scotland at the time of the Second World War.

When We Were Women was first performed at the Cottesloe
Theatre, London, in September 1988. The cast was as follows:

MAGGIE	Mary Macleod
ISLA	Rebecca Pidgeon
ALEC	Henry Stamper
MACKENZIE	Ewan Stewart
CATH/WOMAN	Jan Shand
Director	John Burgess
Designer	Alison Chitty
Lighting	Ian Dewar
Choreography	Dorothy Max Prior

ACT ONE

SCENE I

The back living room, cosy, with a fire and a table and fruit. A mirror over the fireplace. A black fender. It's a room of spit and polish. In the front room there's a full-sized billiards table. This is not a poor house. It's red sandstone and it's big. Nevertheless, its atmosphere is working class. MAGGIE *is dotting around with her coat on over her apron.* ALEC'S *at the fire.* ISLA *is at the table reading a magazine.*

MAGGIE: You could help me, the one or the other of you. The black one. Where is it? Get you up off your great backside. Ma black caiddie. You. You. Sittin' there.

ISLA: Well?

MAGGIE: Where is it then?

ISLA: You don't need it.

MAGGIE: I'm not goin' up that road wi' ma bare head. You're sittin' on it. That's where it is alright.

ISLA: I am not.

MAGGIE: Under your bahoochey. That's where it is.

ISLA: I'm not sitting on it.

MAGGIE: Don't tell me. I've the Police Station to walk by. You're sittin' on it.

ISLA: You'll not be clapped in irons for the lack of a hat.

MAGGIE: Sittin' there.

ISLA: Will you?

ALEC: Get up will you.

ISLA: Eh?

ALEC: Can you no just stand up?

ISLA: If I was sittin' on a hat I'd know. Wouldn't I. I'm not in my dotage.

MAGGIE: And I am I suppose.

ALEC: Hod yer noise.

MAGGIE: I've had about enough of you.

ALEC: Satisfy your Mother.

MAGGIE: Well then.

ISLA: By your foot.

MAGGIE: Eh?

ISLA: Your foot.

(*They look, the two of them,* ALEC *and* MAGGIE.)

MAGGIE: Och. Could you no have said?

(ALEC *sniggers.*)

ALEC: God's streuth.

MAGGIE: You'll not laugh at me. Don't you laugh at me.

ALEC: Och, yer aye goin' off half-cock woman. (*He starts to cough.*)

MAGGIE: Would you listen to him. (*She pours him a whisky.*)

ISLA: Don't give him that.

MAGGIE: A poor cold that's what he's got.

ISLA: Let him be.

MAGGIE: Kills the germs.

ISLA: Pouring that down his throat.

ALEC: That stuff. It'll no kill anything that stuff.

MAGGIE: My own house. My own husband. You'll not tell me how to look after my own man.

ALEC: Have its work cut out for it this stuff.

MAGGIE: You'll not tell me what to do.

ALEC: Away. Away wi' you.

MAGGIE: I've done better than you my girl an' that's a fact.

ALEC: The pair of you. I'll have some generosity between you. The both of you. Do you hear me now? Do you? (*He pours ginger beer into the whisky.*)

MAGGIE: A new hat, that's what I could do wi'. A brand new caiddie. (*She bangs the hat against her leg.*)

ALEC: Bye-bye foam. Wee slip of a thing you were. Sittin' at ma knee. Bye-bye foam. All those years ago.

MAGGIE: Duntin' it's no goin' tae bring it back into the fashion. All the duntin' it's had. Duntin' an' duntin'. All the duntin' in the world'll no save this hat.

ALEC: Bye-bye foam. The years pass. Aye they do. They do that.

MAGGIE: Died long ago this hat. (*Jams it on her head.*)

ALEC: Bye-bye.

MAGGIE: Sittin' there.

ISLA: The tea.

MAGGIE: Do I no look a sight.

ISLA: It'll be made for you to come back to.

MAGGIE: Great hummock on yer front. Sittin' there.

ALEC: Bye-bye foam.

> (MAGGIE *goes*.)
>
> Bye, bye, bye. (*He pours another glass of whisky.*) Here.
> Come here. (*He holds it out to* ISLA.)

ISLA: You never used to drink this early.

ALEC: I'm no drinking now.

ISLA: What do you call this?

ALEC: I signed the pledge for you. Do you mind that? Eh?

ISLA: Yes.

ALEC: The Band of Hope.

ISLA: No that you . . .

ALEC: Aye the years pass. I've always liked a good glass of
whisky. Here. Come on. What do you think. D'you think
I'd ruin a good glass of whisky wi' ginger beer. Would I
commit that sacrilege. I respect him up there, the good
God in his Heaven. What would I do. Would I ruin it. The
greatest of his gifts to man. Come on. Come here. Would I?
Would I do that?

> (ISLA *drinks*.)
>
> Water. She's been waterin' it for years. Water an' a wee bit
> tea. We've had that same bottle since the boys went. I've
> no had a decent glass . . . no in this house. She's a grand
> woman your Mother . . . Thinks I don't know. She canny
> have a large regard for my intelligence if she thinks I don't
> know. A grand woman. I'm damned if I don't think she
> laces it mind. Syrup of figs . . . Every so often I get this
> wee hint of a taste . . . That's what I think she laces it wi'.
> Syrup of figs. Your Mother's answer tae every damn thing
> that is. A cold in the heid tae a bereavement. She's a great
> woman. (*He puts ginger beer in her glass.*) This'll see you
> right. Eh? Bye-bye. Bye-bye foam.

The fire sparks.
There's a street and a man walking up it. No street lights. An edge

of light from one window where the blackout doesn't fit. The sound
of bombs falling here and there. Flashes of light. Firelight.
One loud bang. MACKENZIE *hits the deck in the middle of the*
road. He's in full uniform, with a raincoat over his arm. Quiet.
MACKENZIE *starts to crawl up the road on his belly.*
MACKENZIE: I'll get there if it damn well kills me.

Eh God. If you see what I've got waitin' for me you'd no
send your bombers in.

> Our Father which art in Heaven,
> I am a sinner.
> Hallowed be thy name.
> A terrible sinner.
> Thy kingdom come.
> I humbly ask.
> Thy will be done.

Do not snuff me out. Me. God. Not me. I mean God.
You're a man. God. We're men together God. You and me.
The pleasures of the flesh eh. Soft flesh. Wrap you round. I
bet you've had your fling God. In your time. You've got to
admit it. You were a one. Eh? Eh? And now, eh? Stuck up
there in your nice heaven what have you got left. A pile of
angels. There's no a lot you can do wi' an angel. I mean
when it comes right down to it. God. Looking that's all
you've got left. You're a bit of a voyeur.
(*Bang.*)
Mother Eve see to me. Mother Mary beloved of God hold
me to thy bosom.
(*Bang.*)
Perfumed skin. Powder. Red, red lips. Succour me.
(*Bang.*)
We're no gettin' very far here are we now. I mean look at
me. A more foolish . . . Let me go. Come on. You let me
go an' I'll sin some more for your amusement God. Not
bad sins when you come right down to it. Wee sins in a
minor key. When you consider what could be done.
There's a lot worse sinners than me . . . Aw, come on, man

. . . There's no bloody dignity in crawlin' along a wet road
on your belly.
(*Bang.*)

Give us this day our daily bread.

That's it. That's yer lot. I canny remember the rest of your
prayer God. God. Lord. Lord God. Let me off the rest of
your prayer. Give me one more day to breathe your crisp
clean air.
(*Bang. He covers his head. Silence. The sound of crying. He
lifts his head.*)
You made me. You've got me. Take me or leave me as I
am. God. God.
(ISLA *is sitting by a lamp post.* MACKENZIE *crawls across the
road to her.*)

MACKENZIE: What the hell.
ISLA: I can't see in the dark.
MACKENZIE: What are you doing out?
ISLA: My torch is broken.
MACKENZIE: There's bombs falling from the sky.
ISLA: I've bumped my head.
   (*The all-clear sounds.* MACKENZIE *salutes the heavens.*)
MACKENZIE: Here. Give it here.
ISLA: What.
MACKENZIE: Give me the torch.
ISLA: I walked into the lamp post.
MACKENZIE: That was smart.
ISLA: You're not very sympathetic. My head's sore.
   (MACKENZIE *shakes the torch.*)
   My face is all wet.
   (*The beam comes on.*)
   Am I bleeding.
   (MACKENZIE *takes out a handkerchief and wipes her face.*)
   Is that clean?
   (MACKENZIE *looks at her.*)
   Well?
MACKENZIE: You've a cut over your eye.
ISLA: Do I look awful?

MACKENZIE: What were you out for?

ISLA: None of your business.

MACKENZIE: Manners. Manners.

ISLA: Ow.

MACKENZIE: Sorry.

ISLA: I'm alright.

MACKENZIE: What was so important?

ISLA: I had a bet on.

MACKENZIE: You'll need stitches in that.

ISLA: No one's stitching me. I know you.

MACKENZIE: My God. My God. Covered in blood. It's the Spanish Princess.

ISLA: Eh?

MACKENZIE: I know you.

ISLA: Say that again.

MACKENZIE: What?

ISLA: That. What you called me.

MACKENZIE: Spanish Princess.

ISLA: That's nice.

MACKENZIE: You. You water the beans in that canteen.

ISLA: I do not.

MACKENZIE: Aye you do.

ISLA: I don't.

MACKENZIE: Think you can stand?

ISLA: I can stand.

MACKENZIE: Here.

(*He holds out his hand. She doesn't take it.*)

ISLA: I'm fine.

MACKENZIE: Are you now?

ISLA: I do not water the beans.

MACKENZIE: Where's your hat?

ISLA: I haven't got one.

MACKENZIE: You canny be a lady if you havenie got a hat.

(*Someone lifts the blackout blind behind them. A shaft of light streams out. A voice shouts, 'Aileen'. The light goes out. A figure stands at an open window.* MACKENZIE *grabs* ISLA's *elbow. He takes her into the shadow.*)

No that I'm that fond of ladies mind.

ISLA: Are you not.

MACKENZIE: That's no where my heart lies.

(ISLA *shakes free of him. She tries to walk away. She stumbles. He steadies her.*)

ISLA: I'm alright.

MACKENZIE: I'll see you home.

ISLA: You will not.

MACKENZIE: My old Gran said always to take care of damsels in distress.

ISLA: My Gran said 'Keep your haund on your Ha'penny.'

MACKENZIE: Is that right?

ISLA: I know you. You with your raincoat. You think you're God's gift you do. The lot of you. Don't think I don't know you.

MACKENZIE: Here.

(*He gives her the torch. She walks away. The torch goes out.*)

ISLA: Oh. Oh damn. (*Takes another couple of steps.*) It's no me. The beans. They come like that. The beans. (*Shakes the torch. It doesn't come on.*) I can't see in the dark. (*Shakes the torch. It doesn't come on.*) Please.

MACKENZIE: What was the bet?

ISLA: I'm not telling you.

MACKENZIE: Night. Night.

ISLA: Come here.

MACKENZIE: Well?

ISLA: I want you to take me . . .

MACKENZIE: Night. Night.

ISLA: Please.

MACKENZIE: The bet.

ISLA: Half a pint of gin.

MACKENZIE: Eh?

ISLA: Straight down.

MACKENZIE: Down what. Down where.

ISLA: Well it wouldnie be down the stank would it?

MACKENZIE: You were gonnie drink a half-pint of gin.

ISLA: So what?

MACKENZIE: A whole half-pint.

ISLA: Down in one an' stay standin' up.

73

MACKENZIE: I'll see you home.

ISLA: I don't want to go home.

MACKENZIE: Home.

ISLA: No.

MACKENZIE: What are you? Are you daft? I mean I like alcohol. I'm no sayin' I don't like alcohol. Home.

ISLA: I'm a grown woman.

MACKENZIE: Are you now?

ISLA: I can do what I like.

MACKENZIE: You treat alcohol wi' respect. Look at you. You canny stand up right. I'll get you to your own home if I have to carry you there. And don't you think I can't. I've carried heavier than you. (*He holds out his arm.*)

ISLA: I think I'd be safer wi' the gin.

MACKENZIE: I'll tell you something.

ISLA: What?

MACKENZIE: Right at this very moment you're no that appealing. I mean, when yer cleaned up a bit you might just pass muster. But right now, right now . . .
(*She takes his arm. They walk.*)
Spanish Princess. For your hair an' your hips an' your dark, dark eyes and the way you look at me and your hands wi' their great long fingers an' their red, red nails an' your shoulders an' your shoes an' your white, white socks. See they socks God. Women in white socks God. My God. We're all poor sinners in this vale of tears.

In the room. ALEC *is sweeping at the rug with the brush and shovel from beside the fire.* ISLA's *in the kitchen getting water.*

ALEC: She'll smell it. That's what she'll do. Smell of burning wool. Hangs about. Open up the windaes will you. Wee pit holes in that rug. 'You should have had the fire-guard on.' I'm for it Isla. 'What did you not have the fire-guard on for?' She'll do me. 'You wi' your great feet. That's my good rug.' Pungent. That's what it is, burning wool. There's no getting away from it. Pungent smell that is.

ISLA: It's your rug too.

ALEC: I'll go into the works.

74

(ISLA *comes in with a bowl of water, a bar of soap and a cloth.*)
She'll know. She'll know if it's wet.

ISLA: You can't help a coal fire sparking.

ALEC: That's what it's there for. The guard.

ISLA: You're scared of her.

ALEC: I've lived with your Mother for thirty years.

ISLA: Well then.

ALEC: I've learnt respect.

ISLA: For goodness sake.

ALEC: Your Mother's got a tongue on her.

ISLA: Dad.

ALEC: I've spent my life dodging your Mother's tongue.

ISLA: Pa Pa.

ALEC: I've not heard that . . . Pa Pa.
(ISLA *scrubs at the rug.*)
You learn respect . . . Pa Pa. Not since you were a wee girl. (*He gets his collar and tie. His studs.*) Pa Pa. I'm away into ma work.

ISLA: Pa Pa.

ALEC: Aye.

ISLA: Look at me. (*She stands up.*) You've not looked at me. Not since I came home.

ALEC: My wee girl.

ISLA: Not so very wee.

ALEC: You'll always be that to me. My bonnie lassie.

ISLA: Look at me.
(*He looks.*)

ALEC: Aye.

ISLA: I'm . . .

ALEC: What is it I'm to look at?

ISLA: Pa Pa.

ALEC: I can see you. I can see you.

ISLA: I'll clean the rug.

ALEC: Aye.

ISLA: I could . . .

ALEC: Aye.

ISLA: I could drive you in.

ALEC: Auntie Mac. D'you mind yer Auntie Mac? (*Puts his tie pin in.*) Always askin' for you yer Auntie Mac. Round an' round the place wi' her buckets an' her brooms. Never changes.
(*Cuff links.*) Your Mother worries about the boys. She's a lot on her mind, your Mother. 'How is she then?' says Auntie Mac. Always the same. 'Does she mind the sugar mice? Your wee dark girl.' Auntie Mac never recovered from the day they pulled down the Gorbals Cross. I'll go in by myself. I'll drive mysel' in.

ISLA: Pa Pa.

ALEC: You mind you've got that rug pristine by the time she comes back. Save your old Dad's hide eh?
(*Puts his jacket on. Twists and turns at the mirror.*)
How's that? How's that? Eh? See me when I was young. Cock of the walk when I was young.

ISLA: Pa Pa.

ALEC: Cock of the walk me.

ISLA: The Duke they called you when you were young.

ALEC: Aye an' then they called me the dirty Duke but we'll no dwell on that. My own wee girl. (*And he leaves her.*)

MACKENZIE *lights a lighter. He's waiting near a cinema queue, raincoat draped upon his arm.*

MACKENZIE: Girls (*He lights his cigarette.*) Girls. God. Girls. Rita. Flora. Annie. Annie. Oh my Great good God. No, no. That's it. That's alright. Annie's on someone' arm. Thank you God. Jack. Right you are then. Jack. Annie's with Jack. For a moment there . . . Eh God? Thank you. God. Bless Jack. Keep him safe from all harm. God. Hey God do you see what I see. Mary standin' there. Hey now you've let something slip. You're not taking care of me. Mary standin' there on her own. All, all alone. Hairy Mary in the cinema queue. Come on God. Come on. Come on. Is that fair. That standin' there. Is that fair to a man.
(*ISLA links arms with him.*)
Oh! (*He pats all his pockets.*)

ISLA: What?

MACKENZIE: Wallet.

ISLA: What?

MACKENZIE: Wait.

ISLA: Why?

MACKENZIE: No.

ISLA: What?

MACKENZIE: No wallet.

ISLA: No?

MACKENZIE: Come on.

ISLA: Where are we going.

MACKENZIE: For a walk.

ISLA: We are not.

MACKENZIE: No wallet.

ISLA: I'm not goin' for any walk. I want to see that.

MACKENZIE: No money.

ISLA: I'll pay.

MACKENZIE: I'll have no woman pay for me.

ISLA: I want to see the film.

MACKENZIE: Want doesn't get. (*He walks off, away from the cinema queue.*) I'm not that sort of man.

ISLA: What sort?

MACKENZIE: Eh?

ISLA: What sort's that sort?

MACKENZIE: You're half daft you are.

ISLA: What sort of man are you?

MACKENZIE: Cut it out.

ISLA: I'll slip you the money. No one'll see.

MACKENZIE: No.

ISLA: I want to see the film. I've the money here. What's wrong with me paying? You can give me it back if you're so . . . The queue's almost gone. I want to see the film. The queue's gone in. It's Clark Gable in there.

MACKENZIE: Ah.

ISLA: What?

MACKENZIE: The very thing. (*He pats his back pocket.*)

ISLA: What?

MACKENZIE: Nestled in here. Snug. Safe and sound. Didn't look there. Never thought. I don't keep my wallet there. Pick pockets. Spoils the line of a pair of trousers.

ISLA: You've got it.

MACKENZIE: Daft eh.

ISLA: Have you got a cigarette?

MACKENZIE: We'll miss the film.

(ISLA *puts her hand into Mackenzie's inside jacket pocket. Finds his cigarette case and with it his wallet. She pulls them both out. Tosses the wallet to* MACKENZIE.)

Fancy that.

ISLA: See. Mary. Mary Stuart.

MACKENZIE: Clark Gable's in there.

ISLA: Stuart with a 'u'. Royal Stuart. Well of course Mary's a Royal Stuart. Mary. 'My family's always believed we were by blows of the kings.' Nose in the air. Used to show her knickers to the boys round the back of the synagogue. 'Wrong side of the blanket'. See. I know. I know you. Only ever showed her knickers. Then. I know you're not the clean potato. (*She reads the cigarette case.*) 'To Mackenzie. All my love Rita.' (*Takes a cigarette.*)

MACKENZIE: I don't like to see a woman smoke in the street.

ISLA: 'From Cath.' (*On the lighter.*)

MACKENZIE: Not my woman.

ISLA: I'm not yours. I belong to my own self. Don't you forget it. (*She lights the cigarette.*)

Who's Cath? (*Silence.*) See. I'm not the first woman in your life. Not by a long chalk. I know. But I'm telling you this. I'll make damn sure I'm the last. See that raincoat. You can stop carrying that raincoat. You'll not get me on that raincoat. (*Blackout.*)

SCENE 2

MAGGIE's *walking up to the back door. She's carrying two heavy shopping bags. Her handbag's under her arm.*

MAGGIE: Feel the smell of that. All the way down the lane that's coming. Mrs Paterson'll smell that. Down at number four she'll smell that. The old ladies'll smell that. That's potatoes burning. That's onions burning. That's my good

78

pot. My big pot. (She gets in the back door, lets everything down. Rushes over to the stove. Grabs the pot, the handle's hot. Lifts up the corner of her coat. Uses that to pick up the pot. Rushes over to the sink with it.) What is it that we're having to wur tea tonight. Is it bread we're having. If that's what we're having, that's all we're having. Right down the road I smelt that. What is it? What is it? Is it no enough . . . Do you want them all to know? Showing off your troubles. The waste. We're no so well off that we can afford to ruin good food. Sending your troubles to waft off down the street. Letting them all know. The stink of your troubles. You canny even set a pan of potatoes to boil. Och away an' stop yer greeting. *(She turns on the light.)* What're you sittin' in the dark for? There's dark enough in this world. Greetin' an' greetin'. Where's your pride? Have you no pride? Come on now. Come on. Look at your face. You'll ruin your face. *(She goes over to the table. She wipes the tears off* ISLA's *face with her hand.)* You bathe your eyes in cold water before they all swell up. You're no the only one wi' troubles in this world. We've all got wur troubles. You're no even the only woman wi' a wain in her belly. You're my daughter an' you'll walk through this wi' your head up. I'm telling you. Och would you look at these hands . . . See these hands. Out in that garden wi' these hands I used to make mud pies when I was a wee wain. Same hands. Same hands. I'm a wain yet. Inside. We're all of us wains.

ISLA: 'Keep yer haund on yer Ha'penny.' That's what Gran used to say.

MAGGIE: Aye that's your Gran. That's yer Gran alright. Pity you didn't take her advice.

ISLA: I'm a married woman.

MAGGIE: You. You're no more married than fly in the air. *(She puts the messages on the table.)*

ISLA: How much did you pay her?

MAGGIE: If it'll no be too much strain you can give me a hand. *(*ISLA *doesn't move.* MAGGIE *begins to unpack.)*

ISLA: You're taking advantage of her.

MAGGIE: Hold your tongue.

ISLA: She could go to prison for this.

MAGGIE: I've more than you to take care of. I'll see my children right.

ISLA: My Father lets you do this.

MAGGIE: There's more than me at it. I'll not see my children short.

ISLA: Sixpence. Is that what you give her? Come on. Do you give her sixpence? A nice shiny new sixpence. To herself. Maggie. Maggie. Is that what you give her?

MAGGIE: You'll call me Mother.

ISLA: Ninepence. Is that it? Maggie. Is that her price?

MAGGIE: You'll not address me by my given name.

ISLA: Is it more? Wee Jeannie down at Murray's. Does she come dearer than that. Does it cost you a shilling to get wee Jeannie to bend down behind that counter on a Thursday afternoon. You and all the others. Half-day closing. All of you. How much does she get wee soft Jeannie, to bring out the cheese and the butter an' the bacon an' the jam. Mother. What do you give her?

MAGGIE: You in your righteousness. What do you know about me?

ISLA: The king's shilling.

MAGGIE: I've my big son in a prisoner-of-war camp. Don't you talk to me. (*Pause.*) It's not for myself I'm doing this.

ISLA: And chocolate. You've got chocolate.

MAGGIE: That was for you. (*Pause.*) She gets a good half-crown. Half a crown tae 'ersel'.

ISLA: That'll see her fine when she's in the gaol. That'll see her right an' fine.

MAGGIE: See what she's got put by. I'd like to have what she's got put by. Would I not. Come on hen. My wee hen. Here. (*She pushes the chocolate towards her.*) This stuff. It's all put by for the rich. I'm no depriving any other body. Our boys wouldn't get this, so they wouldn't. It's reserved. To keep 'Them' going. The Hoi Poloi. Why should I no get some. Rich men's cheeses. You talk about risk. I take a risk. Where's the harm. What harm is there? And eggs. I've got eggs. (*She takes the wrappings off a corner of the chocolate.*) A

wee taste. A wee edge. There's iron in that. Feel the smell
of that. You've to take care of yoursel' for the sake of the
wain that's in you . . . A wee piece of that. That'll take the
burning from the back of your throat. That'll clear the
tears away. (*Beat*.) Big brown eggs. (*Beat*.) It's a long time
since you've had chocolate. (*Beat*.) Double yolks they'll
have in they eggs. I'll warrant you that. (*Beat*.) A bit of
chocolate. Do you good. Make you smile. Make you smile.
Do you good. (*Beat*.) We'll keep an egg or two for wursels.
We'll not give them all away. (*Beat*.) I like to see you
smile. (*Beat*.) You see what I'll make you. (*Beat*.) Great
yellow eggs we'll have an' a bit bacon to us. (*Beat*.) You'll
have it made to you. On a tray. On yer knees. At the fire.
An' a bit toast that you can douk in. All cut in soldiers. My
hen. My wee hen. A bit chocolate. Is that not enough to
make you salivate. A nice bit chocolate.
(ISLA *leaves the kitchen*.)
Hen. My wee hen. Isla.

MACKENZIE: Isla (*Beat*.) You can't do it. You can not do it.
(*Beat*.) There's a measure of stupidity coursing with the
blood through the veins of a woman's body. (*Beat*.) Isla.
(*Beat*.) There's a pigheadedness. (*Beat*.) Isla. (*Beat*.) Sheer
pigheadedness. (*Beat*.) Isla. Will you listen to me. I know
alcohol. Don't talk to me about alcohol. (*Beat*.) There's a
bloody mindedness. (*Beat*.) I've seen men clutching at the
chairs to stop them walking round the room. Grown men
wi' blankets over their heads for fear of the beasties in the
dark. That's alcohol. Isla. (*Beat*.) Come on now. Come you
here to me now.
(ISLA *is standing in an edge of light, holding half a pint of
gin*.)
Don't be daft Isla. Pour it away.
(ISLA *laughs*. MACKENZIE *walks towards her*.)
Come on now. Come on now. There's no other body here.
Pour it out.
ISLA: Mackenzie.
MACKENZIE: Pour it away now.

ISLA: Do you love me Mackenzie?
(*There's laughter from behind one of the windows. A radio goes on. There's dance music.*)
MACKENZIE: Don't be so damn silly.
ISLA: Mackenzie.
MACKENZIE: Put that drink down.
ISLA: Do you love me?
MACKENZIE: You'll not drink that.
ISLA: Mackenzie. (*She drinks.*)
MACKENZIE: No.
(*She drinks it down.*)
Oh my God.
ISLA: See. (*Beat.*) Didn't feel a thing. (*She passes straight out.*)
MACKENZIE: Dear God. Good God. Great God. (*He takes her pulse.*) Strange things happen in a war. I have to lift her. I have to carry her. Sweet body. Good body. Come on my Spanish Princess. You canny stay here.
(*He gets her arm round his neck. A voice shouts out from behind the blind with the bleeding light: 'Can you no fix this blind?' Someone fiddles with the blind. Cuts the light out.*)
I am a sinner. (*The arm flops down.*) Anybody could be lookin' here Isla. (*He puts it back.*) I am an evil man. (*The arm flops down.*) Spyin' out. (*He puts the arm back.*) A petty man. (*He tries to take the weight. He can't.*) My God. Will you pull yoursel' together Isla. (*The arm flops down.*) Come on now God. Will you give us a hand here. I mean, no shenanigans. I promise no shenanigans. (*He gets the arm round his neck. It stays.*) Right. Right. All right and tight. (*He heaves her up.*) Right. So far so good. Right. I know what you're thinkin'. I'm gonnie marry this woman. What's wrong with that? What the Hell's wrong wi' that? (*In a light at a bus stop. In the far off distance, a woman (who looks like* CATH) *in a hat and a raincoat, a suitcase at her side.* MACKENZIE *looks.*)
Nemesis. Eh God. Creeping up on me. I'm going to marry her. And why not? There's a war on. I'm going to marry her. Do you hear me? What the bloody Hell's wrong wi' that? (*He walks with* ISLA *in his arms.*)

MAGGIE: (*Yelling up the stairs from the door of the back living room*) Murray's. They make their fair whack out of it. It's a service they're providing an' don't they know it. Don't they charge enough. I've debts. I've bills coming in. What your Faither'll no do to me . . . I've not even got a good hat to my head. Where's the harm? Damn you, Isla, you'll not do this to me. Wee Jeannie's family'll not go short. Isla. What do you think? D'you think they go short? I'm not the only one at it. It's a social gathering up there of a Thursday afternoon. You'd be surprised who I see up there. I'll not tell you who I see up there of a Thursday afternoon. I'll not tell you who's in that queue. Even a minister has to keep his strength up. For the preaching. God's work. Where's the harm? A wee bit lightness. A wee bit bacon. Is it no dark enough? I've your sister to think about. I've her children to think about. I've Moira. I've Ina. I'll not see them short. And the boys. The good God keep them and bless them and send them home. If they come home . . . Oh my God. My dear God. When they come home. I've the boys to think about. And you. I'll think about you. Though you're the bane of my life I'll think about you Isla. Isla.

(*Blackout.*)

SCENE 3

When ISLA *comes to, she's lying on the raincoat.* MACKENZIE *is kneeling beside her. There's a radio on in the background. It's a talk programme.*

ISLA: Oh God.

MACKENZIE: Quiet.

ISLA: What have you done?

MACKENZIE: You passed out.

ISLA: You've taken advantage of me.

MACKENZIE: Eh?

ISLA: I'm lying on it.

MACKENZIE: What?

ISLA: This thing.

MACKENZIE: That's my raincoat.

ISLA: There you are then.

MACKENZIE: Eh?

ISLA: What have you done?

MACKENZIE: Eh?

ISLA: Well?

MACKENZIE: Well what?

ISLA: Have you?

MACKENZIE: Have I what?

ISLA: You know.

MACKENZIE: I don't.

ISLA: Have you?

MACKENZIE: I have not.

ISLA: You have.

MACKENZIE: I have not.

ISLA: You're despicable.

MACKENZIE: I haven't touched you.

ISLA: Have you not.

MACKENZIE: No.

ISLA: I don't believe you.

MACKENZIE: You should know.

ISLA: I wasn't going to end up here. No like the others. All that long line of all they others.

MACKENZIE: No that many.

ISLA: What am I going to do?

MACKENZIE: Yer alright.

ISLA: Am I?

MACKENZIE: For God's sake it's not that bloody appealing making love to a sack of potatoes.

ISLA: I feel terrible.

MACKENZIE: That's your own damn fault.

ISLA: I'm goin' to be sick.

MACKENZIE: No on my raincoat.

ISLA: Serve you right if I am.

MACKENZIE: I haven't done anything.

ISLA: Where am I?

MACKENZIE: Down the back lane.

(ISLA *leaps up*.)

ISLA: Are you daft? They'll all can see.

MACKENZIE: I'm due back.

(*Someone turns the tuner on the radio then switches it off. Silence.*)

ISLA: What do I look like?

MACKENZIE: You'll do.

(*She pinches her cheeks and bites her lips.*)

You could have killed yoursel'.

ISLA: You care do you?

MACKENZIE: What do you damn well think?

ISLA: I'm just that wee bit shaky. Will you give me your arm.

(*She walks off to her own back door. It's open. There's a dull light coming out.*)

Well then.

MACKENZIE: Aye.

ISLA: What?

MACKENZIE: I'll say . . .

ISLA: What?

MACKENZIE: Well . . .

ISLA: Goodnight.

MACKENZIE: What?

ISLA: You'll say . . .

MACKENZIE: Goodnight?

ISLA: Right then. (*She turns to go.*)

MACKENZIE: Isla.

ISLA: Oh for goodness sake.

MACKENZIE: What?

ISLA: You can kiss me.

MACKENZIE: What?

ISLA: That's what you want isn't it?

MACKENZIE: Yes.

ISLA: Well then.

MACKENZIE: What?

ISLA: Come on.

MACKENZIE: Thank you.

(*A kiss. Chaste. A peck.*)

ISLA: What was so hard about that?

MACKENZIE: What?

ISLA: Goodnight. (*She turns to go.*)

MACKENZIE: No.

> (*He grabs her hand, pulls her, whisks her round and down, across, round, running until they stop, kneeling in the light round the crack of a blackout window blind.*)

I, Howard . . .

> (*He behind her. She kneeling in front of him. He cupping her hands in his, crossing them on her breast.*)

ISLA: Who?

MACKENZIE: Take thee, Isla.

ISLA: Not Howard.

MACKENZIE: Sh. Sh. Sh. Sh.

ISLA: Is your name Howard?

> (MACKENZIE *kisses her.*)

MACKENZIE: I, Howard, take thee Isla to wife.

ISLA: You've no got English blood?

MACKENZIE: I vow to love you.

ISLA: I couldnie love an Englishman.

MACKENZIE: Quiet.

ISLA: What?

MACKENZIE: I vow to honour you. I vow to cleave to you. By my word. By my honour. By my truth. As a plain sinner and a man.

ISLA: Are you asking me to marry you?

MACKENZIE: Do you need more than that?

ISLA: What do you mean?

MACKENZIE: We're man and wife.

ISLA: No.

MACKENZIE: In God's eyes. In my eyes. In your eyes. This is our moment.

ISLA: I still feel sick.

MACKENZIE: Isla.

> (*A* WOMAN *stands at an open window.*)

ISLA: I need more than this.

MACKENZIE: Nemesis.

ISLA: In the eyes of the law. In the eyes of the world.

MACKENZIE: Catching up on me.

ISLA: God's in a church.

MACKENZIE: He's up there, just beyond the blackout Isla. I
  know. He's watching me.
ISLA: Mrs Paterson down our road.
MACKENZIE: Will you marry me?
ISLA: The two old ladies.
MACKENZIE: Will you marry me?
ISLA: Aye I will. I will so.
MACKENZIE: Oh God.
ISLA: I'll do that.
  (*She stands in front of him. He takes her hand. Kisses it
  gently.*)
MACKENZIE: Oh my God.
  (*A* WOMAN *further up the road lights a cigarette.*)

MAGGIE:

> Hills of the North rejoice,
> Valley and lowland sing.

(MAGGIE *is singing and frying bacon.*)

> Hark to the advent voice,
> La-la-la-la-la-la,
> Though absent long my Lord is nigh,
> He judgement brings and . . .

The smell of that. Isla. Does that not make your mouth
water? Does that not make your heart sing. Isla. I'm
salivating myself. I've a good fire built up here. Isla. Come
on lassie. You'll not want the bacon to burn. Isla. Don't
tell me you're not hungry. I know you're hungry. A bit
fried bread. That'll do you nice.
  (ALEC's *coming down the road.*)
ALEC: Is that you? Isla? Is it you? Is it? For shame Isla. Where
  are you? Come on hen. My hen. What is it? Eh? Eh? Isla.
  Is it some man? Is it? Eh? Is it some man at you? Eh?
  Remember you're my daughter. Isla. Man. Come here.
  Man. Come on out here. Get your filthy stinking hands off
  her. Come on. Come on. I know men. Do I not? Come on
  now. Eh? Eh? What do you think I'm gonnie do. Do you

think I'm gonnie eat you? Is that what you think? Is it?
Eh? Eh? I'm no gonnie eat you. I'm no. I'm no gonnie eat
you. Eh? Man. Eh? Eh? Eat you? I'm gonnie get my hands
round your damn throat an' I'm gonnie squeeze the life out
of you. I am. I am so. Squeeze the damn . . .

ISLA: You'll wake the whole street.

ALEC: Who the hell's that?

ISLA: Who do you think it is?

ALEC: Is that you?

ISLA: Father.

ALEC: Isla.

ISLA: You're drunk.

ALEC: I am that.

ISLA: Come on.

ALEC: You've no been playing the whore have you?

MACKENZIE: Do you want a hand.

ALEC: Who's he?

ISLA: Mackenzie.

ALEC: Who the hell is he?

MACKENZIE: I want to marry your daughter.

ALEC: A damn sailor.

ISLA: Come on in.

ALEC: No a damn sailor. You're no marryin' a sailor.

ISLA: He's a good man.

ALEC: Is he so. He will be one of the few then.

ISLA: So he is.

ALEC: Are you?

MACKENZIE: What?

ALEC: Simple enough question son. Are you a good man?

MACKENZIE: We all have our faults.

ALEC: Is that right? And what might yours be.

ISLA: Father.

ALEC: Here's a man wants to marry my daughter. I've a
    right . . .

ISLA: Stop it.

ALEC: Aye. Well you've a good face. I'll give you that. A sailor
    wi' a good face. First time for everything. You'll get plenty
    rum then. Eh? Eh? A good sailor. Well. I'll be damned.

MAGGIE:

> Hark to the advent voice,
> Valley and lowland sing,
> Though absent long your Lord is nigh,
> He judgement brings and fealty.

(ISLA's *at the door.*)

I mind when I was in your condition. The hunger. See me when I had you in my belly. Down on my hunkers by this very fireplace. Great big belly I had. Eating coal out the scuttle. An' I'm thinking, 'I don't want to eat this.' But I'm eating it all the same. Ramming it into my mouth I am, so I've got coal dust all down my chin. An' your father comes in an' he thinks they'll be coming to cart me off. 'What do you think you're doing?' he says. An' I smile at him an' I know my teeth are all black. 'What are you, are you blind?' say I. 'I'm eating coal.' An' I'm down there on my hunkers an' I get on my dignity wi' the coal dust all down my chin. 'I'm doing what my body tells me,' say I and I bite into a beeswax candle. One of the tall ones. No that I want to. I don't want to. I want the coal. But I'm showin' him, so I'm munchin' on this candle. 'Guy funny body you've got,' he says. 'It's done you fine well enough,' say I. An' that shuts his mouth.

(ISLA *sits at the table.*)

There's my girl. My lovely girl. Your father. Oh he was a proud man. He was a good-looking man. Before he got his belly on him. (MAGGIE *puts the food in front of* ISLA.) Him an' me on a Friday night. Up the town. Him in his suit. Me in my beads. Parading. That's what we were doing. (*Beat.*) I've more I can make to you. (*Beat.*) We turned many a head. Your father an' me. In wur young days. (*Beat.*) You've got to see to yourself. Take care of yourself. You an' yon wee precious life that's growin' inside you. Don't think I don't know. I know. I know. (*Beat.*) You have your baby. You get it out. Get it done. Then you can start over. Start over. Start over again.

MACKENZIE's *on his own. The* WOMAN *walks up the road. She sees* MACKENZIE. *Stops. Watches him from a distance. Smokes.*

MACKENZIE: Every woman I see. Every woman that passes me. I'm looking under their hats. I'm checking them out. Is it you? Is it? Cath. My love. Smile Cath the world's watchin'. A pair of legs wi' a crooked seam. A clicking pair of heels. Straighten up that seam Cath. I come out in a cold sweat. I need you to take care of me Isla. I'm skulking past policemen. I'm pulling up the collar of my raincoat. I'm going through with this marriage. Do you hear me?

(*The* WOMAN *licks her fingers and straightens up the seam on her stocking.*)

The skies might fall. You'd still have stockings to your legs. Cath. I know. Don't think I don't know. I'm going through with my marriage an' you'll not stop me. I could be dead next week. Scarlet mouth puckered to take a cigarette. You've a cruel mouth Cath. See these hands. See them. Look at the shake on these hands. Shield me Isla. Help me. My Cath has a pair of pelvis bones sticking out that could cut you in two. I'm going ahead with this. Be my wife, Isla. My woman, Isla. My good wife. Love me cherish me. As I love and cherish . . . Keep me safe from harm. One day at a time. One day. Step by step.

(*The* WOMAN *blows out smoke.*)

Step by step by step.

(*She puts the cigarette out.*)

Cath.

(*The* WOMAN *turns. Blackout.*)

SCENE 4

ISLA *sitting at the table, eating.* MAGGIE *watching her. It's breakfast time. There's a ring of the postman's bicycle bell.*

MAGGIE: My God. Did you hear that?

ISLA: What?

MAGGIE: Your Faither's late for his breakfast.

ISLA: What's wrong.

MAGGIE: Go an' get the post for me.

ISLA: What for?

MAGGIE: Run away will you. Go on. Go on.

ISLA: Maggie . . .

MAGGIE: Don't you call me that.

(*The postman's bicycle bell rings.*)

Go on. Go on. It's no much I ask you to do.

ISLA: I'm having my breakfast.

MAGGIE: I'll keep it hot.

ISLA: What's wrong wi' you?

MAGGIE: You'll go an' get the post off the postman an' if your
Faither catches you comin' back you'll tell him you went
down to Sadie's for the bread.

ISLA: I haven't got any bread.

MAGGIE: You'll tell him Sadie was out of bread. You'll not
show him the post. You'll bring the post to me.

(ISLA *sits back with her arms folded.*)

Hurry up. (*Silence.*) Oh my God. Isla. Help me. I'm askin'
you. (*Silence.*) I've bills in the post Isla. I'm askin' for your
help. I canny let your Faither see the bills. He's no got the
money to pay them. An' neither have I. (*Silence.*) That was
a fine big wedding we gave you. (*Noises from upstairs.*)

No that I'm feart of your Faither. Help me Isla. It's no for
mysel' I've spent the money.

ISLA: You'll have to pay some time.

MAGGIE: You look at me. Do I look like . . . I've no even got a
decent hat to go the messages in.

ISLA: He'll have to know some time.

MAGGIE: Did you no hear the ding of that bell.

ISLA: Maggie . . .

MAGGIE: It's only the once your Faither's hit me. For by I spat
in his face. I canny mind what I spat in his face for. But I
mind him hittin' me. He's comin'. Help me.

ISLA: My Faither never hit you.

MAGGIE: Aye he did.

ISLA: My Faither never lifted a hand to you.

MAGGIE: You've always loved him the best. Don't you think I
don't know that. It's easy for a man to be loved.

(*Noise from the bedroom.*)

He's comin', Isla.
(ISLA *gets up*.)
You put those bills in your pocket. You keep your hand on them.
(ISLA *leaves*.)
You keep them deep in your pocket. That's my hen.
You're your Mother's own wee hen. Mind now. Sadie's.
Sadie's for the bread.

There's a WOMAN *out taking the air far off in the darkness, standing, leaning, at her ease.*
ISLA *and* MACKENZIE *are in the torchlight. At the back kitchen door. In the late night.*
ISLA: We'll love each other, won't we. Always. Always.
MACKENZIE: We'll see.
ISLA: Come on Mackenzie. Let's be romantic.
MACKENZIE: Right you are then.
ISLA: You look daft.
MACKENZIE: I'm no a romantic sort of a person.
ISLA: Aye you are.
MACKENZIE: Aye I'm not.
ISLA: You are. You are so.
MACKENZIE: I am not.
ISLA: I know you. (*Silence.*) I do. Don't I. There's no other body in this whole wide world that knows you like I do. Is there? Is there?
MACKENZIE: What do you know?
ISLA: Underneath it all. You're really quite nice.
MACKENZIE: Am I?
ISLA: We'll always tell each other everything won't we.
MACKENZIE: What's this always you keep flinging at me.
You're my woman. I'll tell you what I think it's good for you to know.
ISLA: We'll be honest.
MACKENZIE: Step by step.
ISLA: Give me a kiss.
MACKENZIE: You're daft you are.
ISLA: Are you not gonnie kiss me.

MACKENZIE: You should marry some fine young chap wi' a cushy number an' prospects.

ISLA: I don't like fine young chaps.

MACKENZIE: Marry a right bastard an' you get what's comin' to you.

ISLA: I don't like that word.

MACKENZIE: I'm sorry.

ISLA: I'll not have bad language.

MACKENZIE: Isla . . .

ISLA: Mackenzie . . .

MACKENZIE: I could be dead next week.

ISLA: Cross your fingers an' pray to God when you say that.

MACKENZIE: I'm praying alright.

ISLA: Do you really want me?

MACKENZIE: Aye. I do.

ISLA: Well then.

MACKENZIE: What?

ISLA: That's alright, then.

MACKENZIE: Aye.

ISLA: As long as you want me.

MACKENZIE: Aye. I do that. I want you alright.

(*The torches go out and the* WOMAN *in the far distance shivers in the cold, turns up the collar of her coat and goes home.*)

ISLA *slams the bills down on to the table.* MAGGIE *looks at them. Each one of them. Then she stuffs them down into the pocket of her apron.*

MAGGIE: See you've got to keep things from them. You've got to keep your own counsel. Never give yoursel' away. Keep a bit of yoursel' private.

ISLA: What'll you do with them.

MAGGIE: I'll handle your Faither in my own time. I'll see to him.

(*Blackout.*)

SCENE 5

The wedding day. ALEC *is filling a hip flask from a bottle of rum. He's half-dressed in morning dress, in his shirt sleeves and his waistcoat. Whistling and singing.*

ALEC:

> Oh I will take you home Cathleen,
> Across the Ocean wild and wide,
> To where your heart has ever been,
> Since first you were my bonnie bride.

(*He pockets the hip flask. Stands at the mirror over the fire tying his tie. A dove-grey cravat. Pins it with a golden pin.*)

> The roses all have left your cheeks,
> I've watched them fade away and die.
> Your voice is sad when e'er you speak,
> And tears bedim your loving eye.
> Oh I will take you back Cathleen,
> To where your heart will feel no pain,
> And when the fields are fresh and green,
> I will take you to your home again.

(ISLA, *in her wedding dress, stands at the door.* ALEC *sees her in the mirror. Turns to look.*)

Aye.

ISLA: Is that all you've got to say.

ALEC: My bonnie lass. My bonnie wee lassie. Here. (*He gets out the hip flask.*)

> I'll give you a toast in good Navy Rum. You'll not ask me where I got it. May you be as happy through the years as your Mother and I have been. (*He drinks.*) If you can do that you'll be doing well. Here. (*He hands her the flask.*) That'll set you up.

ISLA: Pa Pa.

ALEC: My bonnie lass.

ISLA: I wanted to say . . .

ALEC: Drink.

(*She shrugs and swallows.*)

94

You could always take a drink well. If I've taught you
nothing else I've taught you that. My own wee girl. My
own. My ain one. You were always your Pa Pa's best girl.
My dark princess. My wee girl sitting at ma knee . . . (*He
sits down.*) Come on. Come here.
(*She sits on his knee.*)
Cheeky wee thing you were. You in your red dresses. Your
mother always had you done up fine. Your wee red boots. I
like to see a woman dressed. I'm that proud of you. You've
been a good girl. A good, good girl. Don't you tell me you
haven't had the opportunity to be otherwise. I know. I
know men. Don't I just. We've got wur faults. We're good
creatures at the bottom but faults, we've got faults. I know
what I'm talkin' about. Your Mother an' me we could
always trust you. We've always been proud of you. You've
kept your goodness. That's a fine thing. It's a pure gift
you've got to give to your Mackenzie an' I know he
appreciates it. He's a rare good man. A gift, that's what it
is you're bringing to him. The greatest gift a woman can
give to a man. An' he'll know. You'll belong to him. Only
to him. You listen to your old Faither. I'm proud of you.
You're giving him your goodness. (*He takes hold of her chin
and strokes her cheek.*) Not that I'm drunk. I'm no drunk.

ISLA: I know.

ALEC: You'll no find me drunk this day. If I drink your health
now an' again that's all I'll do.

ISLA: I don't . . .

ALEC: A man has his disappointments Isla.

ISLA: I know you . . .

ALEC: A man can drink his own daughter's health on her
wedding day.

ISLA: You do what . . .

ALEC: Can he not? Eh? Can he not?

ISLA: We'll drink the one to the other. (*She gets off his knee.
Toasts him with the hip flask.*) Here's tae you.

ALEC: Mind your Mother now. That was a different tale. My
Maggie. My wicked Maggie. No virgin bride in all her
innocence my Maggie. Walked up the aisle carrying her

95

hummock in front of her, carrying it for all to see. Dressed in white an' smilin' to either side. Daring them, any one of them to say a word to her. Daring God hissel'. My Maggie. My wicked Maggie. She'll go to Hell my Maggie. God'll never smile on her as he's smilin' on you this day. Did she no lay wi' me on the Isle of Millport. She cam' away on her holidays wi' me. Seventeen years old. Defyin' them all. I took your Mother on a train. You take my meanin'. I took her. Scrappy affair it was. Us both wi' wur clothes still on. Down the corridor, between the carriages, on a train to Millport. You've your gift to your husband. You've the gift of your own sweet self, on your wedding night. My wicked Maggie. See I never knew. If I . . .

(MAGGIE *behatted at the door.*)

MAGGIE: You're the one and only love of my life. That's what you are.

ALEC: Am I so? Am I that so?

MAGGIE: Have I not made you my whole life.

ALEC: Tell me Maggie. Tell me.

MAGGIE: Your back collar stud's undone.

ALEC: I don't know.

MAGGIE: Come here an' I'll see to it.

ALEC: I don't know.

MAGGIE: Have I not brought up your children to be whole and good.

ALEC: You were that headstrong Maggie.

MAGGIE: I've brought them up right.

ALEC: Was it me?

MAGGIE: Does it matter now?

ALEC: For if you did it with me like that. There on that train wi' the draught blowin' roun' wur bare parts . . .

MAGGIE: I've been your wife these twenty-seven years.

ALEC: Could you not have gone wi' any other man.

MAGGIE: It was war time.

ALEC: War time then.

MAGGIE: Strange things happen in a war.

ALEC: War time now.

MAGGIE: So many never came back.

ALEC: Was there more than me? You're aye a good-lookin'
woman Maggie. You're my torture Maggie.

MAGGIE: I've always loved you.

ALEC: Always.

MAGGIE: Did I not pay enough for that dress to be made right.
You get away from yon fire. You'll have it burnt before the
day's right started.

ALEC: My wee girl.

MAGGIE: She's not your wee girl.

ALEC: I've an hour or two yet.

MAGGIE: She's a woman grown. Let me look at you.

ISLA: I wanted to say thank you to you both.

ALEC: What have you got to thank us for?

MAGGIE: Turn round.

ALEC: You've nothing to thank us for. The greatest gift God
gives on to the earth is a child to love. You've been a child
both lovely and loving.

MAGGIE: You're beautiful so that's alright.

ALEC: Blessed little children. Blessed, blessed children. I've
watched you grow. You've made me proud.

MAGGIE: This is your day.

ALEC: Bless you.

MAGGIE: We've done wur best for you.

ALEC: Bless you.

MAGGIE: See an' enjoy your day.

ALEC: Seeing you in that.

MAGGIE: It needed taken in . . .

ALEC: I mind your Mother in that.

MAGGIE: A wee bit taken in . . .

ALEC: Seventeen year old.

Dance-band music from the wedding reception.
Maggie's voice singing 'My love is like a red, red rose'.
MACKENZIE's *on his own. Leaning. Taking the air.*
MAGGIE:

> Till a' the seas gang dry my dear
> An' rocks melt in the sun

Oh I will love thee still my dear
While the sands of life shall run.

(*A* WOMAN *walks down the street.*)

MACKENZIE: Cath. Cath. Cath. (*He's speaking to the* WOMAN *as she walks.*) My dead brother. Cath. What that did to me. Eh? What did that no do to me? Cath. I'll not say we didn't have good moments. Cath. Look at me. Photos of me. They'll be doing this day. Do I not look fine? Spruced up and immaculate. Spit an' polish. She's a good girl. Cath let me be. My brother. I thought we were charmed the pair of us. Cath. We're none of us charmed. Cath. Stay away from me. Cath. Cath.

(*The* WOMAN *stops as she gets to him.*)

WOMAN: Are you talking to me?

MACKENZIE: Cath.

WOMAN: I'm afraid you must be mistaken.

MACKENZIE: I beg your pardon.

WOMAN: Please . . .

MACKENZIE: I'm sorry I . . .

WOMAN: Could I have a light?

MACKENZIE: Of course . . .

WOMAN: Look at your hands.

MACKENZIE: What?

WOMAN: Are you cold?

MACKENZIE: No.

WOMAN: You're shaking.

MACKENZIE: I've been married this day.

WOMAN: That's enough to make a body shake.

MACKENZIE: My wedding day.

WOMAN: Congratulations. Thank you. (*She holds out the lighter.*)

MACKENZIE: What?

WOMAN: Cath eh? (*She's reading the name on the lighter.*) Is that your wife. (*She gives him it back.*)

MACKENZIE: You need more than a good moment or two.

WOMAN: That's right.

MACKENZIE: In a life.

WOMAN: Why not.

MACKENZIE: That's right.

WOMAN: Good luck to you. (*She walks off.*)

MACKENZIE: Cath.

WOMAN: No. Not me.

MACKENZIE: You have to grab at life. That's what I say. Grab
and hold hard.

WOMAN: That's right. That's very right.

MACKENZIE: Cath. Damn you Cath. It's my wedding day.
Here.
(*The* WOMAN's *walking away.*)

WOMAN: Not me son. Not me.

MACKENZIE: Do you want this? (*The lighter.*)

WOMAN: Eh?

MACKENZIE: You take this.

WOMAN: Why?

MACKENZIE: I've had my use out of it.

WOMAN: I can't . . .

MACKENZIE: I want you to have it.

WOMAN: Why not?

MACKENZIE: For luck.

WOMAN: After all.
(*She takes the lighter.* ISLA's *in the doorway.*)
Good fortune.

ISLA: They're wondering where you are.

MACKENZIE: Aye.

ISLA: Who were you talking to?

MACKENZIE: Some woman.

ISLA: Come an' dance.

MACKENZIE: In a minute.

ISLA: Are you sorry?

MACKENZIE: What?

ISLA: You're not sorry?

MACKENZIE: Here.

ISLA: Why?

MACKENZIE: Come here.

ISLA: You come here.

MACKENZIE: Where did you get to be so . . .

ISLA: What?

MACKENZIE: Insolent Madam. That's you. Cheeky wee besom. That's you.

ISLA: Who was she?

MACKENZIE: I'm going to catch you.

ISLA: Why were you talking to her?

MACKENZIE: I'll get you.

ISLA: Mackenzie.

MACKENZIE: Run.

(*He catches her. Tickles her.*)

ISLA: No.

MACKENZIE: I've got you. I've got you.

ISLA: I'm your wife.

(*He stops.*)

MACKENZIE: Isla. (*He's holding her.*)

ISLA: What is it? (*Beat.*) Mac. What?

MACKENZIE: I've a present for you.

ISLA: I like presents.

(*He reaches into his inside pocket. Gives her a small black leather Bible.*)

That's a very serious present. (*She opens it.*)

Forever and always. That's a long time. What a long, long time.

The WOMAN *with the cigarette lighter lights a cigarette in the far, far distance.*

The dance band in the hall playing 'Red Sails in the Sunset'.

MAGGIE's *in the doorway, drinking and singing.*

ISLA *and* MACKENZIE *dance. Round and round and round. The circle of their dance widens. When they reach the* WOMAN, *the dance stops.* MACKENZIE *takes the woman in his arms and* ISLA *watches.*

ALEC: Dance wi' yer old man. Come to my arms wee hen.

(MAGGIE *watches and sings on.* ISLA *and* ALEC *dance.*)

You'll do well to let him be. I see your eyes. I know what you're thinking. It's a wise woman that knows when to keep her mouth shut. For a man to marry is a great thing. He's giving up everything. A woman now that's a fair different story. A woman, she gains everything. Position. A place in the eyes of the world. On her finger for all to see she bears the mark of being wanted, the mark of her belonging. A ring. It's what she's been brought up for. The summit of her amibition. The goal of all her training. Look. See him dancing there. Do they not look well together? Aye, she can dance. She can dance alright. Look how they move the both of them. What if he strays. What if? You let him be. You smile an' he'll come runnin' back. Mind me what I'm sayin' now. Mind. These words are the gleanings of the years. I've learnt. I'm wise. Oh yes I'm the wise one. Mind me. Mind what I'm sayin'. He's a fine big man. An' you've caught him. That's a great thing. Now you break him in gently. Be canny. Never nag. Give him that much freedom he never knows he's been caught. Keep his meals hot an' his bed well aired. Keep yersel' pure for him. An' mind you wear some perfume of an evening. Mind that. There's nothing like the smell of a woman's perfume. Mind all that an' he'll come home to you and he'll bear with him armfuls of flowers an' a heart full of gratitude that he'll lay at your feet. Gratitude'll hold a man longer than any youthful idea of love. Gratitude's what makes a bond. And guilt. I know. Do I not know. Love now. Love. That merely makes the marriage. You smile my wee girl. Smile. Smile. Let your beauty shine forth on this glorious day. For you've made your old Father a happy, happy man.

(*Blackout.*)

ACT TWO

SCENE I

The light is on MACKENZIE *in the darkness. He's wearing a navy-blue greatcoat.*

MACKENZIE: I'm on the deck. I've ropes all round me. Lyin' there. Ropes as thick as a wrist. Ropes thick as a man's thigh. All round me. It's cold. Cold. Cold. I'm lookin' up. The sky's flat grey an' the sea's all empty. I'm alone. I've no gloves an' my hands are chapped. Where's my God damn gloves. Some bugger's pinched them. My hands are chapped wi' the cold. I've had boils in my beard an' the doctor's said my blood's bad. I'm a sinner. What does he expect? An evil man. Eh? Eh? The sea's empty an' the sky's empty. And I thank you God. Me standin' there in amongst the ropes on yon cold deck. I thank you God for the empty sky. I can see hope in an empty sky.

MAGGIE:

> I to the hills will lift mine eyes,
> From whence doth come mine aid.
> My safety cometh from the Lord,
> Who Heaven and Earth hath made.

MACKENZIE: I've the phones on. I'm listening. There's nothing. I'm that quiet. I'm that still. God you know I'm a Heathen deep down at the bottom of me. But I'm a good Heathen. You know that. I've the phones on my ears. All is silence. Thank you God. There's no bloody subs this side. Thank you, God. Boom. You've filled the world for me. Boom. Boom. You've exploded a bloody torpedo in my eardrums. Come on play the white man. Where was the bloody sub God. Come on. Come on. Boom. And my world's all red. Boom. Easy come, easy go. Eh God.

MAGGIE: Bring my boys back. Bring my boys safe back to me.

The sun's shining. ISLA *and* MACKENZIE *are sitting on the raincoat, looking out over the Firth of Clyde.*

MACKENZIE: You canny call these boats.

ISLA: I'll call them what I like.

MACKENZIE: There's no dignity in a boat.

ISLA: They're floating aren't they.

MACKENZIE: Big bloody things like that lying at their rest in all their majesty. These are ships, woman, ships.

ISLA: You'll not get me on one.

MACKENZIE: Scotland's glory these are.

(*The* WOMAN *is in the distance.*)

ISLA: Who's that?

MACKENZIE: Welded, riveted, fitted. Right here. Right here.

ISLA: She's lookin' at us.

MACKENZIE: I like the sea. I love the sea. I'll be a sailor all my life.

ISLA: She knows you.

MACKENZIE: When this war's over an' I've seen it through I'll join the Merchant Navy an' you'll be a sailor's wife an' you'll come wi' me an' we'll visit the far-flung corners of this world. You an' me Isla. You an' me.

ISLA: Who is she Mac?

(MACKENZIE *looks at the* WOMAN. *She comes towards them.*)

MACKENZIE: Just some woman that's all.

(*The* WOMAN *stands above them. Floats a newspaper cutting down into* MACKENZIE's *lap.* ISLA *picks it up.*)

ISLA: That's us. That's our wedding photo. Do I know you?

CATH: Your landlady told me where to come.

ISLA: The old one?

CATH: Aye.

ISLA: Peggy that'll be. I don't know you.

(MACKENZIE *yanks* ISLA *to her feet. Pulls at her to get her away.*)

What is it? What is it?

(*He starts to run, holding on to her.*)

Your raincoat, Mackenzie. (*She breaks free of him. Runs back. Picks up the raincoat. Runs back to* MACKENZIE.) My God, Mackenzie. What is it?

(*He grabs her hand.*)

MACKENZIE: Come wi' me. Come wi' me. (*He starts to run.*)

ISLA: You're hurting me.

(*He's pulling her along with him.*)

MACKENZIE: Isla.

ISLA: You're hurting my hand.

(*He runs with her. She stumbles and falls. He catches her, holds her in his arms.*)

MACKENZIE: Guitars. You an' me. Eh Wilf? Singin' for wur supper. Tiger Bay. What the Hell we were doing there. Brat you were. Right there. Right there beside me. I'll take care of you wee lad. I'll see you alright. Has my sin been so great Lord. My good Lord. Take a look around you. Take a good, good look. You tell me why you're cursing me. Eh Lord? My wee brother in the sea clinging to his life. My wee brother. He liked the girls. My great good Lord up there in your fine Heaven. What was the harm my wee brother did unto you that you should kill him there in that cold sea.

(*He jerks* ISLA *to her feet.*)

Get up. She's behind us yet. Come on.

(*He drags her behind him, running still.*)

ISLA: I can't run any more.

MACKENZIE: Come on.

ISLA: I've no got the shoes for it.

MACKENZIE: Take your damn shoes off.

ISLA: I can't run in my bare feet.

(MACKENZIE *shakes her.*)

MACKENZIE: Run will you. Run will you. Run. Run.

ISLA: She knows where we're staying.

MACKENZIE: We're no goin' back there. (*Beat.*) Come on. Come on. (*Beat.*) Don't greet. Dinny greet.

ISLA: You're hurting me.

MACKENZIE: Move will you woman.

ISLA: Who is she? (*Beat.*) We canny keep just running.

MACKENZIE: There Isla. There. There, there, there.

(*He wipes her face with his hands.*)

No time for that now.

(*They run on.*)

ISLA: What is it? What is it?

MACKENZIE: Come on.

ISLA: Who is she?

(MACKENZIE *stops.*)

Who is she?

MACKENZIE: She's my wife.

ISLA: Don't be daft. (*Silence.*) Oh my God.

(MACKENZIE *sits down.*)

I'm expectin'.

MACKENZIE: Are you.

ISLA: It's early days yet. I've a baby in me.

MACKENZIE: I'm sorry.

ISLA: All that runnin'. (*Beat.*) What's her name?

MACKENZIE: Cath.

ISLA: An' she's your wife.

MACKENZIE: Aye.

ISLA: Have we stopped? Is that it? Have we stopped running
now? She's your wife? (*Silence.*) What does that make me?
And the wain that's inside me. What am I?

In the back room. ALEC *stands over the table.* MAGGIE *is sitting
there.* ALEC *holds his hand out.* MAGGIE *looks at him.* ALEC
bangs the table with the flat of his hand. MAGGIE *digs her hand
into her apron pocket. She brings out the bills. She hands them to*
ALEC. *He looks at them. He hits her. About the shoulders. She
takes it.*

ALEC: You've shamed me.

(*He leaves the room.* MAGGIE *leans on the table with her head
on her arms.*)

On the hill above the Firth of Clyde, in the sunshine, MACKENZIE,
CATH *and* ISLA *are sitting side by side by side.*

ISLA: It's a beautiful view. You really can't beat the view.
There's no other country can beat Scotland. I've always
said that. If we had the weather. If we just had the
weather.

CATH: I've two kids. Tam's six and Jackie's three.

said that. If we had the weather. If we just had the
weather.

CATH: I've two kids. Tam's six and Jackie's three.

ISLA: It's a pity about the weather.

CATH: Jackie's my love. She's like her father. A right wee
charmer. She's his eyes.

ISLA: He's a handsome man.

CATH: And curls she's got.

ISLA: Has she?

CATH: Of course she's dark.

ISLA: And you've children.

MACKENZIE: They're no my kids.

CATH: Don't you start that. Tam's quite the wee man. Six years
old an' he's got his boats all lined up an' he can tell you the
frigates an' he can tell you the destroyers.

ISLA: Ships aren't they.

CATH: A right wee man. Cock of the walk he is. Like his father
before him. (*Silence.*) It wasnie clever to put the picture in
the paper.

MACKENZIE: D'you think I did that?

ISLA: My Father was that proud.

CATH: What did you think was gonnie happen?

MACKENZIE: I hate you. May God forgive me.

CATH: He might. I'll not. I'm gonnie get you Mackenzie. If I
have tae go so far as to have you put in the gaol then that's
what I'll do. I'm gonnie get you for what you've done to
me. I'm sorry for your woman don't you think I'm not. But
I'm no gonnie think about her. I'm gonnie think about
mysel' an' my wains an' I'll get you.

ISLA: Would you excuse me. I have to be going now.

MACKENZIE: Stay where you are.

ISLA: Oh no please Mackenzie you must see I . . .

MACKENZIE: You're no the one should leave.

ISLA: Let me go.

(*Blackout.*)

SCENE 2

MAGGIE's *sitting at the table. The light from the hall's shining into
the room.* ISLA's *standing at the sink in her underwear. She's
washing and washing and washing her body with a cloth. Washing
on top of the underwear.*

MAGGIE: A woman has to cleave to a man. That's what I say. A
    woman has her man. A woman needs her man. I'm with
    your Faither. I'm with him yet. Don't you think we've not
    had wur troubles. We've had wur troubles. A wee quarrel.
    You'll have plenty of those through the years. At least let
    me put the light on. You're a married lady, you're not
    some wee girl. The ring you've got on your finger. That's a
    blessed thing that ring. You'll no sin against that ring.
    (*Beat.*) Ma wee hen. Will I no put the light on? Isla. You'll
    spoil your nice . . . your Father could come down here.
    Isla. Let me put on the light. (*Beat.*) What is it? What is it?
    I'll have no trouble in my family. Not in my family. If we
    had on the light. I don't want you down with a cold.
    (ALEC's *at the door.*)

ALEC: What's the noise?

MAGGIE: Cover yourself.

ALEC: This time of night.

MAGGIE: D'you hear me?

ALEC: A man's his work in the morn.

MAGGIE: Get yourself covered.

ISLA: Look at me.

MAGGIE: What is it? What is it?

ISLA: Look at me.

MAGGIE: I've my nice dressing gown here.

ALEC: It'll be her condition. That'll be what it is. Maggie.

MAGGIE: I'll not have this trouble in my house.

ALEC: You wi' your first wain. You were maudlin.

ISLA: Look at me. Look at me.

MAGGIE: We're lookin'. We're all lookin'. An' a right eyeful
    that's what we're gettin'. Where's your modesty. Is your
    Faither no a man right enough that you should strip
    yoursel' under his eye. Alec you'll get away to your bed.

ALEC: A wee cup of tea. That's what she wants. Plenty of sugar. She keeps a good house your Mother.

MAGGIE: You've yer work.

ISLA: Look. Look at me. Look at me.

ALEC: A wee dram.

MAGGIE: I'll deal wi' it.

ALEC: She'll catch cold.

MAGGIE: Get to bed.

ALEC: Wettin' all her parts like that.

MAGGIE: Go on. Get. Get.

(ALEC *goes.* MAGGIE *picks up the dressing gown and puts it round* ISLA.)

Letting your father see you like that. Your body. Your breasts sticking out through. Giving him his eyeful right enough.

ISLA: Look at me. Look at me. Look at me.

(MAGGIE *slaps her.* ISLA *stops.*)

MAGGIE: Have you no shame. Sit down. Sit down.

(ISLA *sits at the table.*)

There's no excuse for this. None whatsoever. You're a grown woman.

ISLA: I'll not go back.

MAGGIE: Giving your father a red face.

ISLA: I can't go back.

MAGGIE: Don't talk nonsense.

ISLA: I'm soiled by him.

MAGGIE: A good night's sleep.

ISLA: He's made me dirty.

MAGGIE: Sleep's what you need. Sleep's all you need.

(*There's a knocking at the back door. Silence.*)

There you are.

ISLA: No.

MAGGIE: For goodness sake.

ISLA: It's him.

MAGGIE: This time of night.

ISLA: Don't let him in.

MAGGIE: Don't talk daft.

ISLA: Please Mother.

MAGGIE: Thank the good Lord you've a man that'll bother tae come chasin' away after you.

ISLA: Mother.

MAGGIE: There's many a many wouldnie bother their heads.

ISLA: I can't talk to him.

MAGGIE: There's a handkerchief in the pocket of my dressing gown. Dry your eyes. Here.

ISLA: I'm that ashamed.

(MAGGIE *reaches into the pocket.*)

MAGGIE: Here. That's it. Never let a man think he's got the better of you. Blow. A good blow. That's my girl. Now. (*She opens the door.*) Aye. Come away in. Come you away in. I don't know what's between you. I don't want to know. I mind my own business. Sit down.

(MACKENZIE *sits at the table.*)

Now you. The both of you. You make your peace between you. For your own two sakes. For the wain's sake. I want no trouble in my house. (*She stops at the door.*) Mind an' keep yer noise down. I've my man asleep up the stairs. (*Silence.*) Right you are then. (*She goes.*)

ISLA: My Father's got his work tomorrow.

MACKENZIE: Of course.

ISLA: She worries about him.

MACKENZIE: Aye.

ISLA: He drinks.

MACKENZIE: I know.

ISLA: Mind he's a nice drinker. There's no harm in him. Poor wee man. No harm at all. I'm gonnie break his heart. If I'd lain wi' you on that raincoat. We'd not be in this mess, would we? Would we?

MACKENZIE: I don't know.

ISLA: Virtue is it's own reward. Is that not what they say? She thinks he's all she's got left.

MACKENZIE: Does she?

ISLA: Mind she's wrong about that.

MACKENZIE: Is she?

ISLA: She's got me hasn't she? (*Pause.*) Hasn't she?

MACKENZIE: I suppose . . .

ISLA: Me an' the wain.

MACKENZIE: Isla . . .

ISLA: Inside my belly.

MACKENZIE: I love you.

ISLA: Don't.

MACKENZIE: It's the truth.

ISLA: A brat I've got in me. Your brat.

MACKENZIE: Please . . .

ISLA: Your bastard. (*She spins the ring on the table.*) I've got my
Mother.
(*They both watch the ring spinning.*)
You could have taken me on your damn raincoat. I'd have
succumbed eventually. Don't we all. Don't we all lie flat on
our backs and part our legs for you. (*She catches the ring.*)
Will she divorce you. Mackenzie. Will she?

MACKENZIE: She's a Pape.

ISLA: I see.

MACKENZIE: I was a boy when I married her.

ISLA: Is that right?

MACKENZIE: I made a mistake.

ISLA: Oh well.

MACKENZIE: I love you.

ISLA: Uncle Keir kissed that ring. Uncle Gordie blessed it.
Auntie Ann wet it with her tears.

MACKENZIE: It's dark.

ISLA: I like the dark.

MACKENZIE: I'm scared of the dark.

ISLA: And you a big man.

MACKENZIE: Let me put the light on.

ISLA: Never show a man yer whole body bare. My Mother told
me that. Keep your secrets. Never show a man all yer
body.

MACKENZIE: As long as I pay her we'll can live together. She'll
not tell.

ISLA: You've children. Mackenzie. Oh God. Oh God.

MACKENZIE: There's not a soul'll know outside the three of us.

ISLA: God'll know.

MACKENZIE: There'll be no difference to us. You'll have a ring to your finger.

ISLA: I'll have that.

MACKENZIE: I'll never leave you.

ISLA: Will you no.

MACKENZIE: We'll be alright then. The two of us. You an' me.

ISLA: God looks down.

MACKENZIE: We'll can go on as we are.

ISLA: I don't want the light on. I don't want the light on at all.

CATH *outside by the window lights the lighter, lights a cigarette.*

MACKENZIE: If we were not meant to take our pleasure, the women and the men. What for did You give us the tools to take our pleasure with.

(MACKENZIE *takes a light from the lighter. Lets it burn. Takes* CATH *in his arms.*)

> Jesus bids us shine with a pure clear light,
> Like a little candle burning in the night,
> The world is filled with darkness,
> We can make it shine,
> You in your small corner,
> And I in mine.

(*Snaps the lighter out. Holds* CATH *tight.*)
We're in the water Cath. Him an' me. Wilf. (*Beat.*) It's dark. An' I'm yellin' 'Where are you son? Wilf.' (*Beat.*) I'm callin' him. 'Wilf!' (*Beat.*) Listen. Listen. (*Beat.*) Nothin'. (*Beat.*) My wee brother, Cath. (*Beat.*) Nothin' (*Beat.*) Listen. (*Beat.*) I'm alone in the water. They've killed my brother Cath. Does that no deserve punishment? (*Beat.*) Clear eyes he had an' a twinkle. And I was to look after him. D'you mind his drawings. Cath. Cowboys wi' cigarettes hangin' out the corner of their mouths an' wee dogs peein' up against lampposts. What I've done to you. It's very small beer indeed.
(*She lifts her head from his shoulder. Looks at him.*)
Will you let me be.

(*She moves out of his arms. Silence. He catches her hand.*
Holds it hard.)
Will you put me in the gaol? Will you do that? (*Silence.*)
Aye. Alright Cath. Alright.
(*Blackout.*)

SCENE 3

MACKENZIE: Hey You. You. Did You take a wee nap was that
it? Poor old Fella. An awful lot's expected of you. Keeping
up the natural order. What were you doing? Did you take a
wee break. Were you watchin' them dancin', the Daughters
of Men? Right nice wee things. Eh? And all your own
work. Guitars an' they waggle their hips. Look there. Look
there. The wee one wi' the lips an' the ukulele. Can she no
sing. Take care of her. Keep her safe from harm. A wee
toy to grace your universe. We're all of us toys. Eh? Is that
not right?

MAGGIE *and* ISLA *are in the back living room.*
ISLA: My lamb. Kicking at my ribs. My lamb. Making me take
notice. Turning over inside of me. Making me go on. It an'
me. You'll not take my child away from me. My very own.
You've not got the right to take my child from me.
MAGGIE: You've to make a new life for yourself.
ISLA: My life's here in me.
MAGGIE: You'll find another man.
ISLA: We belong together, it an' me.
MAGGIE: You were bonnie before.
ISLA: I don't want another man.
MAGGIE: You're bonnie yet. You need a man. Too bonnie for
your own good. You'll want one. You'll want one alright.
ISLA: Don't tell me.
MAGGIE: You'll not get one wi' a wain hangin' at yer breast.
ISLA: I know what I want.
MAGGIE: An' me. Eh? What about me? Eh? What about what I
want. Eh? Answer me that. Do I no get a look in? What do
I want? Playin' the fine heroine. You wi' yer face straight

an' never a smile about yer mouth these dark days. What about me? We could all do wi' a smile. I've seen it, the scorn in your eyes. I've seen it. Don't you think I haven't. You an' yer Faither. I can't go into a shop now . . . He's . . . Your Father . . . He's taken my pride from me. An' you're askin' me. Askin' me. Tendin' to a wain. Years at a wain's beck an' call. I've my own big son in prison camp in Germany. I'm tired. I'm very, very tired, I get by. Day by day by day, I get by. I've your brother on the submarines. My mind's full up. There's not the room inside my head to take on another thing. Isla. Are you listening to me? Isla. I pray. I'm walking round here. I'm cooking, I'm no here. I'm cleaning. I'm all the time talking to God. I'm keeping my sons alive. I'm that long on my knees at the side of my bed in the night. I'm talking to God. I'm talking and talking. I've no room in me for a baby. We make our own way. I've no time. Each one of us, our own way. I've no room in my heart. Make your own way. I'll not tend it for you. I'll not care for it. Make your own way. I'll not look after it. Make your own way. I've had five wains of my own. I'll not start over. I can't.

ISLA: It'll not go on for ever, the war.

MAGGIE: I'm that tired.

ISLA: You'll take care . . .

MAGGIE: You're no listenin' to me.

ISLA: You'll take care of my baby for me.

MAGGIE: There'll be war an' more war. And I'll tell you why. Men. That's why. Men are sinners and God's in his wrath.

ISLA: I'll go out to work.

MAGGIE: If I could just sleep.

ISLA: I'll not take money from you. I'll pay for my keep. Take care of my baby for me.

MAGGIE: Men are sinners and the good God is sick at the stench of them. I'll get the tea.

ISLA: Blood of your blood.

MAGGIE: I've a nice bit sliced sausage. Och listen hen. There'll be other babies. Aye you're lookin' at me. It's the truth I'm tellin' you an' one day you'll thank me for it. What's it gonnie be like for him eh, a wee bastard living down this road an all they folk knowin'. There's always babies.

ISLA: You'll keep my baby for me.

MAGGIE: It's a boy you're carryin' there. I know from the way it hangs. It's a boy you're bringin' into the world.
(ALEC *comes in from work*.)

ALEC: See here what I've brought. See here what I've got for my wee girl. My own wee girl. (*He puts a Scottie dog ornament on the table*.) What some people throw out for junk. That's no junk. That was in the old man's shop round the corner from the works. Sittin' there all forlorn. We'll give that house room. We'll give that a home.

ISLA: Pa Pa.

ALEC: See its tartan collar.

MAGGIE: Tea.

ALEC: It's a bitter night.

MAGGIE: It's good an' hot.

ALEC: It'll want livenin' up.

MAGGIE: Is that right?

ALEC: I'm cold to my bones.

MAGGIE: Are you now?

ALEC: Look at yer dog hen. A rare wee dog. If I had a dog.

MAGGIE: Dirty things. Dogs.

ALEC: That's the dog I'd have.

ISLA: I can type.

ALEC: A wee drap. A wee, wee drap.
(MAGGIE *gets the whisky*.)
Is there no some of that rum. Aye. A wee touch. An' a wee touch more.

MAGGIE: It'll run out of the cup.

ALEC: Tip out some of the tea woman. Can ye no.

ISLA: I've a head for figures.

ALEC: A good education my family's had. They'll not hold that against me. Not any one of them. I've seen to their education.

ISLA: I can earn my living.

ALEC: What is it that you want hen?

ISLA: I can pay for my keep.

ALEC: You tell your old Pa Pa.

ISLA: I can work.

ALEC: So you can.

ISLA: Pa Pa.

ALEC: A good cup of tea.

ISLA: My keep an' my baby's.

ALEC: Warm the cockles of your heart.

ISLA: Please.

ALEC: Are you no gonnie look at your dog hen. That I brought home for you. To cheer you.

ISLA: Help me.

ALEC: Yer nice wee dog hen. (*Silence.*) I'm no sayin' I don't understand . . .

MAGGIE: Men are children Isla. Take that to your heart and keep it there. In pain we bear them. God's cursed we are. And pain they give us all the long night through.

ISLA: No.

ALEC: I'm no the one that's got tae look after it.

MAGGIE: I'm telling you.

ALEC: She's a good woman your Mother.

ISLA: I want to keep my baby.

ALEC: A good strong woman.

ISLA: 'Anything you want', that's what you said to me. 'I'll get you the moon from out of the sky if you ask me for it.' Pa Pa.

ALEC: I'll bide by your Mother's decision.

ISLA: God help me.

ALEC: That's it finished. I'll hear no more.

ISLA: You've talked about this.

MAGGIE: We're man and wife.

ISLA: The two of you.

MAGGIE: A woman cleaves to her man.

ISLA: And he holds to her.

ALEC: I've seen them lookin' at you. You walkin' down the street. You've kept yersel' nice. I'll grant you that. There's many a woman would have let hersel' go. I've seen them lookin' at you. Sorrow at their mouth an' a smile in their eyes. You send that child away. Peepin' out frae behind their curtains. I've seen them. An' you wi' yer head held high. An' your misfortune. My own proud girl. Send that child away. These folk. We live amongst these folk. Send that child where it'll have a good life. Do that for it. 'Shame,' they're sayin'. 'Shame. Shame.' An' they're shakin' their heads an' they're hidin' their smirkin' faces behind their hands. 'Shame. Shame.' I'll not have my daughter held up to this. Nor my wife. Nor any grandchild of mine. I have to walk down that street too. This is where I live. All my life I've lived here. This street knows me. It's seen my joy. It's seen my despair. I started the works in my own back yard. I'll bide by your Mother's decision. I walk down that road an' I'm naked. And don't you think they'd forget. Them behind their curtains. They've long memories. Long. Long. And your wain, he'd feel it too. You've all my love, wee girl. All my love. You give that child away. All my love. You make a good marriage for yousel'. Listen to me, what I'm sayin'. Find some rich man. Marry some big doctor. Someone that'll take you. Someone to belong to. That'll still their waggin' tongues. Marry. Marry well. Make them laugh on the other side of their damn faces.

ISLA: Please.

ALEC: Listen to yer Faither.

ISLA: Help me.

MAGGIE: I'll not look after your child.

ISLA: Mackenzie. Mackenzie.

ALEC: You can't get blood out of a stone.

ISLA: You'll not give us house room.

MAGGIE: No.

ISLA: You'll not even do that. Is this not my home.

ALEC: Your Mother's had enough.

MAGGIE: You stay. You. Stay by all means. Stay as long as you want. An' welcome.

ISLA: I see.

MAGGIE: I'm sorry hen.

ALEC: We're aye that.

MAGGIE: I say my prayers for you.

ALEC: The both of us.

ISLA: Thank you.

ALEC: We're sorry alright.

MACKENZIE: Heart beating? Yes. Spine intact. Legs. Yes. It's
    dark. I'm cold. Why's it so God damn dark? Pulse. Yes.
    My eyes. Can I see? Give us a light in your God damn
    world can't you. God? Don't leave a man to grovel here.
    Bowels moving. God no. Don't take my dignity. I'm
    scared. God save me. Now I lay me down to sleep, I pray
    the Lord my soul to keep. If I should die before I wake I
    pray the Lord my soul to take. Light God. Light. Thank
    you God. God bless you sir. I can see fine well. I always
    had a good pair of eyes. There's many a many has fallen for
    my eyes. Eh God. I'm your boy. Oh God. Look there God.
    Look there. That's my wee brother there. God. Were you
    so busy? You never paid him any mind. That's my wee
    brother dead over there.

ALEC *has a telegram in his hand.* MAGGIE *takes it from him. He
stands there. She reads the telegram.* ALEC *sits down at the table.*
MAGGIE *puts the telegram carefully up on the mantelshelf. She
stands by* ALEC *and cradles him in her arms.*

MAGGIE:

> Abide with me,
> Fast falls the eventide,
> The darkness deepens,
> Lord with me abide.
> When other help has fled,
> And comforts flee,
> Help of the helpless, oh,
> Abide with me.

(*Blackout.*)

SCENE 4

MACKENZIE: Terrible kind of self-pity about me now. Always was. Touch of the maudlin about me. That hacked body lyin' there. Men go from this man's navy. Men walk. Disappear. Not me. I havenie got the guts. God. You missed something out when you made me.

> My cup's full and running over,
> For the Lord made me,
> I'm as happy as can be.

> Stand up, stand up for Jesus,
> Ye soldiers of the cross,
> Lift high his royal banner,
> It must not . . .

> My cup's full and running over.

Flesh. Warm. Firm to the touch. Warm skin under my hands. I'm a good man wi' a woman. Grant me that. I've had plenty practice. My hands on my dead brother's body. Laid my hands on him an' the flesh gave back when I touched him. Clammy. Sick dead flesh. And I left him there. Free will. Eh God. We're all of us free agents in this best of all possible worlds.

MAGGIE's *bending over the fire. She's about to throw a letter in.* ISLA *catches her.*

MACKENZIE: We all have wur excuses. Eh Lord?

ISLA: No.

MAGGIE: The fright.

(ISLA *grabs her wrist.*)

MACKENZIE: What's yours?

ISLA: Give me that.

MAGGIE: I've had about enough of you.

ISLA: You've been burning them.

MAGGIE: For the best.

ISLA: My letters.

MAGGIE: I did it . . .

ISLA: How many?

MAGGIE: . . . for the best.

ISLA: How many?

MAGGIE: It was your Faither that started it.

ISLA: My letters. (*She sits at the table.*)

MAGGIE: Aye well.

(ISLA *reads the letter.* MACKENZIE *stands at the table with her. Not there.*)

MACKENZIE:

> Isla,
> Not so bad here. Not so very bad. They feed me that's the main thing. I like my food. I'm to get out soon. Back on the ships. Back on the convoys. Russia they say. I want to ask. Would it be a cheek to ask. Can I see you? I have to ask, can I please see you? I've written an' I've written. You called the wee lad Grant. That's a fair good name. Your Mother wrote to me. She says he'll carry that name. The folks he's gone to. They'll give him that name. My poor, poor Isla. Let me see you. Forgive me.
>
> Cath came the once. Sweet Cath. Let her vile tongue wag at me. Claimed I had my just deserts. What I did I did out of love for you . . . Don't you hate me now. I couldn't stand that. Look at me. I'm a poor thing. I'm not worth your hatred. A frightened man. That's all I am.
>
> At some future time. I'll let you know when I'm out. When I get leave. Where I'll be. I need to know you forgive me. My love goes to you for ever and always.

(ISLA *scrunches up the letter and throws it on the fire. Puts on a jacket, picks up a bag and walks out. Blackout.*)

THE BRAVE

CHARACTERS

FERLIE	A Scottish woman in her mid-thirties
SUSAN	Her sister
JAMIE	An engineer
ROBERT	His friend
HOCINE	A barman
A POLICEMAN	
A MAN	

The Brave was first performed at the Bush Theatre, London, in June 1988. The cast was as follows:

FERLIE	Eleanor David
SUSAN	Kate Lynn-Evans
JAMIE	Maurice Roeves
ROBERT	Gregory Floy
HOCINE/	
POLICEMAN	Tony Osoba
A MAN	Danny Cerqueira

Director	Simon Stokes
Designer	Robin Don
Lighting	Rick Fisher
Sound	Martin Warr

ACT ONE

SCENE I

A swimming pool in the moonlight. The water's glistening. The stars shine down. God's in his Heaven and the world's just fine.
A man lies stretched out. Prone. Eyes closed. Immobile. Amber prayer beads tight in his hand. A woman, solicitous, bends over him. Out of the moonlight and the music of the spheres comes FERLIE'*s voice. She's been talking and talking and she goes on talking.*

FERLIE: You're going to feel awful sorry about this in the morning. The head you'll have in the morning. (*She takes a silk handkerchief out of his top pocket. Dabs at his face with it.*) No that I'm not sorry. Oh Christ. *Pardonnez moi. Je m'excuse.* (*She puts the handkerchief to the back of his neck.*) My sister'll know how to deal with you. My sister's in the loo. My sister's a woman of action. Jesus. (*Her voice gets louder and louder.*) I'm not some wee lassie lookin' for love under a great big moon. This is a Muslim country for God's sake.
(*The* MAN *rolls his head. Groans.*)
Shhhhh. Shh.
(*Her hands fly to his mouth. Fly to her mouth. She looks round in fear of someone coming. The* MAN *doesn't move. She crouches next to him. Whispering. Gossiping. Still looking around her at the hotel rooms above the pool. At the bar. At the pool itself. And back at the corner of the bar, where the palm plants are and there are chairs, the shadow of a man moves, wakes from a drunken sleep. Wakes slowly. Stretches there, sheltered amongst the palms. Becomes conscious of* FERLIE'*s voice chattering on. Shrinks into himself and listens.*)
At home. See. *Chez moi.* We've got this park right up the road from us. Nice park it is. I've two children. There's deer in the park. They love the deer, my kids. We fed one once. Great big thing it was. Antlers all over the place. Course we shouldn't have really. I mean. They're dangerous, deer. But it had a nice kind look in its big

brown eyes. All of a sudden there starts to be rapes in the park.

(*The* MAN *on the ground shifts. Groans.*)

I don't want you to think that I think that you were going to rape me. No. No. No. I wouldn't think that. The thought never entered my head. *Comment allez-vous?* (*She chaffs his hand.*) I was standing here lookin' at the moonlight, for God's sake. That's all. (*She pokes him.*) I was polite. That's all. (*She pokes.*) You've got to be polite. I was brought up to be polite. Eh? I can't abide rudeness. Come on. Come on. (*She lugs at him a bit.*) She's an awful long time in the loo. My sister. (*She lugs at him. He doesn't move.*) We all stopped going to the park. Deserted, it was. The rapes stopped. *Pas aucune . . .* rape. It's a bit rusty, my French. Well, I mean, they would, wouldn't they . . . stop. No one there. Then we all got cross. In our local church hall. *Dans l'église nous sommes en coleur.* Where the pop groups practise an' they have the Woodcraft Folk. The Woodcraft Folk are gonnie take over the world. You know. We got this man. Look I think you can move if you really try. *Essayez.* Black pyjama things he had, an' a big red cummerbund. *Essayez.* We had to salute him all the time. Bow. Call him Master. *Le Maître.* He'd watched too much telly. (*Beat.*) Jesus. Where is she? (*Beat.*) He said it was all part of the discipline, the master thing. Calling him Master. He was a bit of a podge really. (*She lugs at him.*) Please. (*She lugs at him again.*) This is some night.

(*The* MAN *does not move.*)

You should get up on yer own two feet an' move around. I know you're embarrassed, well I am too. So that's the both of us. (*She lugs at him.*) I've never known anyone so long at the loo. (*She lugs at him.*) Och. Jesus. Jesus. (*Beat.*) This podge in the black pyjamas, he taught us self-defence. So we could all go back to the park. We did quite well.

(*The* MAN *groans. Opens his eyes. Heaves himself up on to his elbows.*)

There you are now.

(*The* MAN *looks.*)

D'you want a hand up.

(*The* MAN *looks*.)

My friend Beth. She was the best at it, Beth. Beth figured it was the man in the black pyjamas. The rapist. The Master. Private enterprise, she said. Drumming up trade. It's a Tory borough. (*Beat*.) Och I . . . Take my hand. (*Beat*.) We all got back to the park. Please. (*She holds out her hand*.) Mind this is the first time I've had a chance to use it. I'm a pacifist. Still it's nice to know it works, don't you think after all that practice. (*Beat*.) Come on. Come on now. You take my hand. Heads. You've got to be careful wi' heads.

(SUSAN *comes back from the loo. The* MAN *groans mightily. Collapses back*.)

SUSAN: Oh my God.

FERLIE: He's alright. He moved. He did.

SUSAN: What the Hell's wrong with him? (*Beat*.) Is he drunk? Is he. (*Beat*.) Ferlie?

FERLIE: You were that long . . .

SUSAN: What happened?

FERLIE: He moved. Honest he did.

SUSAN: Well he's no movin' now. (*Beat*.) Ferlie?

FERLIE: I was assaulted. (*Pause*.) Near raped I was. (*Pause*.) I was.

SUSAN: How the Hell did you manage that?

FERLIE: I needed you.

SUSAN: For God's sake.

FERLIE: What the Hell were you doin' in the loo?

SUSAN: What did you do to him?

FERLIE: What did I do? What did he do?

SUSAN: Come on Ferlie.

FERLIE: I didn't do anything.

SUSAN: Don't be so . . .

FERLIE: What? What?

SUSAN: Ferlie.

FERLIE: I threw him. That's what I did. Over my shoulder. I did.

SUSAN: What?

FERLIE: And he went down and I hit him. With my keys. To make sure. Just the way I've been taught.

SUSAN: Oh my God.

(*She bends down to the* MAN. *Takes his wrist. The prayer beads dribble out from between his fingers.*)

FERLIE: I only meant to stop him.

SUSAN: Did you?

FERLIE: I didn't mean to hurt him.

SUSAN: He's a Muslim. (*She touches the beads.*)

FERLIE: He's a rapist. That's what he is.

SUSAN: He's half-dead. Not to put too fine a point on it. Och Ferlie.

FERLIE: What was I supposed to do?

SUSAN: This is a sick man.

FERLIE: What do you mean?

SUSAN: His pulse is weak.

FERLIE: Don't be stupid. (*She bends down beside* SUSAN.) Here you. Come on you. Get up on your feet. Pull yersel' together.

SUSAN: Ferlie.

FERLIE: You're not a doctor. What do you know. Setting yourself up . . . Oh God. Was I supposed to let him?

SUSAN: Don't be so daft. Give us a hand.

FERLIE: You.

SUSAN: What?

FERLIE: Right up your street this.

SUSAN: Eh?

FERLIE: Direct action. Aren't you proud of me?

SUSAN: Jesus Ferlie, you don't take direct action against a Muslim in the country of his birth. Jesus Ferlie, you were never subtle.

FERLIE: You can talk. You can bloody talk.

SUSAN: Take a hold of his feet.

FERLIE: I could do wi' a cuddle at the very least from my own sister. What was I supposed to do.

SUSAN: Take his feet.

FERLIE: I couldnie let him rape me.

SUSAN: You overreacted.

FERLIE: What?

SUSAN: Keep your voice down.

FERLIE: I need a friend. That's what I need. I need a friend and I get you.

SUSAN: Come on will you.

FERLIE: You didnie see what he was doing to me.

SUSAN: We're taking this man to your room. We're doing it now.

FERLIE: You were in the loo.

SUSAN: Keep your voice down and pick up his feet.

FERLIE: I defended myself.

SUSAN: When I say lift you bloody well lift before some other body gets here an' scuppers us properly. This is not Largs.

FERLIE: What am I gonnie do wi' a man in ma room.

SUSAN: You're gonnie take care of him.

FERLIE: I don't want a man in ma room. I came here for a rest.

SUSAN: You're gonnie make damn sure he doesn't die.

FERLIE: He cannie . . . Don't be so stupid.

SUSAN: Lift.

FERLIE: A wee bump on the head.

SUSAN: Ferlie.

FERLIE: We should get a doctor.

SUSAN: Eh?

FERLIE: We should. We should so.

SUSAN: He'll ask you questions. The doctor. What are you gonnie tell him? The doctor?

FERLIE: The truth. I'll tell him. (*Beat*.) Susan?

SUSAN: You're all in one piece. You've not a mark on you. There's not even a rip in your clothes.

FERLIE: Slip him some . . . what do you call it . . . baksheesh, d'you call it? The doctor. That's what they do. Isn't that what they do?

SUSAN: You did this with your own hands. You did this deliberately and with malicious intent.

FERLIE: I did not.

SUSAN: Prove it.

FERLIE: He needs a doctor.

SUSAN: And what about me?

FERLIE: Oh God.

SUSAN: I've got to watch myself. Ferlie please.

FERLIE: Oh God.

SUSAN: I can be thrown out of this land. (*Pause.*) I've nowhere
to go from here.
(*Pause.*)

FERLIE: Oh God Susan you should have taken me to your flat.
This wouldnie have happened if you'd a taken me tae yer
flat. Jesus. We canny shift him.

SUSAN: No doctor.

FERLIE: You canny shift head cases.

SUSAN: What do you suggest? (*Pause.*) It's prison you're facing.

FERLIE: You'd know all about that.

SUSAN: Take a hold of his feet.

FERLIE: I'm a Foreign National.

SUSAN: Lift.

FERLIE: It wasnie my fault.

SUSAN: One, two, three.

FERLIE: I've two wee kids at home.

SUSAN: Lift.
(*Between them they carry the* MAN *away.*)

FERLIE: Oh God.
(JAMIE *glints out of the shadows. Watches.*)

JAMIE: Well. Well. Well. Well. Well. Well. Well.
(*Blackout.*)

SCENE 2

Bright morning by the pool. ROBERT *strums Hawaiian songs on his
guitar. Above the pool is the balcony and shuttered door of Ferlie's
room.*

FERLIE *is standing at the wall on the sea side. She's wet.* JAMIE
swoops down on her. HOCINE, *the barman, hovers in the heat.*

JAMIE: It's nice in the sunshine.

FERLIE: What?

JAMIE: Better in the moonlight.

FERLIE: Sorry.

JAMIE: You'll be tired.

130

FERLIE: What?

JAMIE: I'll just bet you're tired.

FERLIE: Well . . .

JAMIE: Watch your feet in that sand.

HOCINE: (*Cutting in*) We have a beautiful swimming pool.

FERLIE: Yes.

HOCINE: So.

FERLIE: We've a leisure centre back home with waves.

(JAMIE's *looking at her*.)

Course it's not the same.

(JAMIE's *staring at her*.)

Not that I swim in it. It's a fine big pool. All that wee-wee. Well . . . I don't swim in it.

HOCINE: Your feet in the sand . . .

FERLIE: You never know what you might catch. That's what I say.

(JAMIE's *staring and staring*.)

There's only you today is there.

HOCINE: By the water's edge . . .

FERLIE: Just you an' this great big pool.

HOCINE: Come over the wall.

(JAMIE *goes on staring*.)

Let me help you.

FERLIE: Just you to take care of all this big pool.

HOCINE: We are short of staff.

FERLIE: Are you?

HOCINE: You must not swim in the sea.

FERLIE: Why are you?

HOCINE: There are scorpions in the sand.

FERLIE: Are there?

HOCINE: Scorpions lie in the cool sand at the water's edge.

FERLIE: Really.

HOCINE: This is their habit. An inadvertent foot and . . .

FERLIE: Yes. (*She scrabbles over the wall. Scratches at her feet.*)

No wonder you're short-handed.

HOCINE: *Comment?*

FERLIE: Oh God.

HOCINE: Already two are dead at Zeralda.

FERLIE: An' the guests here.

(SUSAN *comes in past the bar, carrying a rose de sable.*)

Have you lost any guests from . . .

SUSAN: Ferlie.

FERLIE: Scorpions there are in the sand.

(JAMIE's *staring again.*)

HOCINE: The Fates have smiled upon you.

FERLIE: I must have missed that.

SUSAN: Coffee please.

FERLIE: It doesn't feel like they're smiling to me.

SUSAN: Coffee.

JAMIE: (*Shouting over*) You're a wee smasher. D'you know that?

SUSAN: What're you doing down here?

FERLIE: He's sleeping. The Rapist.

JAMIE: A right wee smasher.

FERLIE: Or he's dying.

SUSAN: For God's sake Ferlie.

JAMIE: Here's tae you.

FERLIE: He snores a lot.

SUSAN: Sh. Sh. Sh.

JAMIE: Here's tae me.

FERLIE: I couldn't sleep.

JAMIE: Here's tae us.

FERLIE: He wet the bed.

JAMIE: Wha's like us?

SUSAN: Don't cry. For God's sake don't cry.

FERLIE: If you hadn't gone to the loo . . .

SUSAN: You're a grown woman.

FERLIE: He smells of garlic. He smells worse an' worse.

SUSAN: If I can't leave you alone for ten minutes.

JAMIE: Slange ladies.

FERLIE: He's awful sick.

JAMIE: Slange.

SUSAN: Who is that man?

FERLIE: He keeps lookin' at me.

SUSAN: What is it? What is it? What makes you think that
every man in your immediate vicinity has designs on your
unquestionable virtue.

FERLIE: This isn't what I grew up for.

SUSAN: You've been the same all your life.

FERLIE: When I was wee an' I had dreams, this wasn't what I saw.

(*The guitars strum.*)

SUSAN: Did he not open his eyes?

FERLIE: He needs a doctor.

SUSAN: Did he not speak.

FERLIE: I want to go home.

SUSAN: Did you look in his pockets?

FERLIE: I don't like it here.

SUSAN: Who is he?

FERLIE: There's scorpions on the beach.

SUSAN: Don't step on them then.

FERLIE: I'm not goin' back to that room.

SUSAN: You've brought this on yourself.

FERLIE: What?

SUSAN: Nothing.

FERLIE: Me an' him an' the walls an' the sound of the bloody sea.

SUSAN: Smiling.

FERLIE: Jesus, the noise of the sea.

SUSAN: You're a liability do you know that.

FERLIE: I couldn't sleep Susan. I couldn't sleep.

SUSAN: Violence is a political weapon.

FERLIE: Waves to and fro . . .

SUSAN: It's not an ureasoned . . .

FERLIE: . . . to and fro.

SUSAN: . . . response to . . . Violence is a platform. It has to be thought through.

FERLIE: I did think. I thought an' thought an' while I was thinkin' he got his hand right up my skirt an' he had the zip on his trousers undone. While I thought he was half throttling me.

SUSAN: Oh God Ferlie.

FERLIE: He was violent. Him. Him.

SUSAN: Smile.

FERLIE: I was brought up to be pleasant and I am, I am.

(HOCINE *puts the coffee on the table by the pool. Because he's there the women smile and smile.*)

I'm very, very pleasant. That's all I know.

SUSAN: Smile.

FERLIE: What am I gonnie do?

SUSAN: Trust me.

FERLIE: I'm not a violent person. Not really.

SUSAN: You're overfond of being liked.

(HOCINE *fusses by the table and the women smile.*)

FERLIE: If you cannie be pleasant. People, the one to the other. What else is there? I don't want him to die.

SUSAN: Smile.

(HOCINE *is very close.*)

See the present I've bought you. Look at the lovely present. This is a rose de sable. The desert's only flower. Smile at the rose de sable. Smile damn you. Smile.

FERLIE: I've got dry teeth.

SUSAN: We're gonnie take this rose de sable up to your bedroom.

FERLIE: I'm no goin' back up there.

SUSAN: Smile.

FERLIE: My lips are sticking to my teeth.

SUSAN: Come with me.

FERLIE: No.

SUSAN: Keep smilin'.

FERLIE: I'm no comin'.

SUSAN: Smile. Smile.

FERLIE: I'm no.

SUSAN: Give me the key.

FERLIE: We can dump him in the street. I don't want him in my room any more. Smellin' up the place. Wi' his garlic an' his breathin'. In the dark. I don't care about that man. In the street. They'll find him. Someone'll find him. There's lots of bodies there. I saw. Comin' in from the airport. I saw the bodies. All they bodies. That's what we'll do. When it's dark. Then it'll be alright.

SUSAN: There's always bodies in the street. Anywhere you go there's bodies in the street. It's only in a foreign land you assume there's dead bodies in the street. It's a natural prejudice. There's policemen in the street and they've got guns.

FERLIE: Oh God. Oh God Susan. What if he dies.

SUSAN: Give me the key to your room.

(FERLIE *gives her the key.*)

Be a good girl.

(SUSAN *goes up to the bedroom with the rose de sable.* FERLIE *sips the coffee.* HOCINE *appears at the table with a refill and whisks a fly from* FERLIE's *arm with a napkin, brushes sand from her feet.*)

FERLIE: The pools of my youth. They weren't like this.

(*The guitars strum on.* FERLIE *talks, chatters – fast, relentlessly. The closer* HOCINE *comes, the more* FERLIE *chatters, the louder, the faster. Laughter in her voice, a smile on her face and her whole body shrinking away from his touch.*)

Well. Not in Glasgow. Not precisely like this. I like to swim in the sea. Changing rooms all round the pool there were. No daylight. A skylight way high up, all covered wi' pigeon slime. The sun doesnie reach through that. One day for the boys. One day for the girls. An' all they tiles. (*She corrects herself.*) Those tiles. Those.

(HOCINE *sits beside her.*)

I came out here to find some peace. Mary Anne McGeachy used to pinch my socks. I hated her. (*She tries politely to hint him away.*) D'you know I'm hungry. I'm very, very hungry. I've never been so hungry.

(HOCINE *stays where he is. Smiling.*)

Mary Anne McGeachy used to pinch my socks in Calder Street Baths. My sister used to beat her up for me. Hold her under the water. Didn't help. (*Beat.*) I could eat cheese. I could fair go a bit of cheese. And ham. And some bread. I'm ravenous. (*Beat.*) Violence only makes things worse. This is what we find. Then I got older an' Mary Anne McGeachy, she'd pinch my suspender belt an' I'd leave the pool wi' ma stockings rolled round my ankles. An' all the class would laugh, an' my sister, she'd laugh too. An' all the boys on the bus when I went home they

were laughing at me. I came out here to find some peace.
That's a laugh. Does that no just make you curl up. (*Beat*.)
And bread. I could eat a mountain of bread.
(HOCINE *brushes sand from her shoulder*.)
Stockings with seams they were. Them that wore no seams,
they were tarts. Dirt line high up on the tiles. Grey an'
green an' slimy. Calder Street Baths. An' the water. Cold,
cold, cold. It's a dark place, Scotland. Poor, poor Scotland.
Course this is not what you're interested in. I know what
you're interested in. All of you.

HOCINE: May I?

FERLIE: What?

HOCINE: Some last small piece of sand. (*He brushes her cheek
with his finger*.)

FERLIE: I haven't eaten since the plane last night.

HOCINE: You must not burn.

FERLIE: Skin like a rhinoceros me. I really am awful hungry.
I'll not burn.

JAMIE: You've got tae watch they wops. No like an honest
Scotsman.
(HOCINE *rises*.)
Oh aye. Oh aye.

ROBERT:

> Driftin' an' dreamin'
> While shadows fall

(HOCINE *retires behind the bar*.)

> Softly at twilight
> I hear you call.

(*He teases with the guitar*.)

JAMIE: See you.

ROBERT:

> Love's old sweet story . . .

JAMIE: You're a worried woman.

FERLIE: I'm on holiday.

ROBERT:

    Told with your eyes.

FERLIE: I'm hungry.

JAMIE and ROBERT:

    Drifting an' dreamin'
    Sweet paradise.

FERLIE: You can fairly sing.

JAMIE: My voice isnie now what it once was. It's no been the same since I got my false teeth.
(*The shutters bang in Ferlie's room above the bar.* FERLIE *looks up.* SUSAN *is at the window.*)
I've been watching you.

FERLIE: Why? (*She drags her eyes back from* SUSAN *up there at the window. Tries to smile.*)

JAMIE: I wanted to be an Opera singer but my Mammy didnie have the money tae get ma voice trained. The Toad Choir an' the ukulele, that's what I got.

FERLIE: My Mum an' Dad used to sing. (*But her eyes are up at the window still.*)

JAMIE: It's a terrible thing when you lose yer teeth. Sit for hours over an electric bar fire, I would, mouth wide open gettin' the heat at my gums.

FERLIE: My Dad's got his greenhouse now.

JAMIE: We're workin' on the revival of Hawaiian music me an' him. We know them all. This is Robert. I'm the talker. He's the silent type with the heart of gold an' the wallet full of the paper stuff. You keep lookin' up there.

FERLIE: My room's . . .

JAMIE: Eh?

FERLIE: Sorry?

JAMIE: You're married.

FERLIE: Yes.

JAMIE: Pity. (*Beat.*) Orphans of the desert me an' him. Pipe linin'. (*Chord on the guitar.*)

    Nobody's child
    I'm nobody's child.

Orphans of the desert. Workin' half naked, drippin' wi' sweat. I'm in ma singlet an' my boxer shorts. Cuttin' my life short. I'm a white man. Is this what I'm meant for? I wear a towel roun' ma neck tae catch the sweat. Ten minutes out on site I'm wringin' the damn thing out. The romance of the desert. Another ten minutes I'm wringin' it out again. Pipe linin'. Four days every six weeks we get. Four days on the town for the sake of wur sanity. Is that what you're here for?

FERLIE: What?

JAMIE: Your sanity?

FERLIE: I came to . . .

JAMIE: Four days tae tank up on precious liquid so we can sweat it all out again.

Nobody's child.

Workin' for the Arab to rob him of his shekels. Mind he's a canny beast the Arab. Don't feel sorry for this emergent nation. Slap a penalty clause on the contract. You work your bollocks off to bring it in on time. They hold up your equipment in the dock. Don't let it through customs. You can't work. They invoke the penalty clause. You end up paying them for the privilege of working for them. An' all you get for your troubles is the Queen's Award for Industry an' a hearing in the bankruptcy courts. Coinin' it abroad. That right Robbie?

Nobody's child.

Robbie's gonnie be a millionaire by the time he's forty-five. No that long to go Robbie. An' the youngest man ever to be a Labour Prime Minister wi' all his hair in. That's where it's at, eh Robbie? Robbie is sufferin' from schizophrenia. He's a Marxist capitalist sitting in a socialist country being screwed by capitalism. Hence the Hawaiian music. See if Robbie canny be a socialist prime minister an' I'll tell you frankly he's the wrong class, when it comes right down to it Robbie's common . . . if Robbie canny be a socialist prime minister he's gonnie don a wig, a grass

skirt an' some coconut shells an' do Hawaiian drag in all
the gay capitals of Europe. If he doesnie meet a good
woman first. Are you a good woman?

FERLIE: What?

JAMIE: You're lookin' up there again.

FERLIE: She's a long time.

JAMIE: I could do wi' a wee shower. Take the sweat an' grime
from off my body. Make my skin soft for the adventures of
the night. Eh?

FERLIE: I must . . .

JAMIE: Must?

FERLIE: I . . .

JAMIE: Must what?

FERLIE: I must . . .

JAMIE: You're aye shiftin' woman. What is it wi' you?

FERLIE: Sorry.

JAMIE: An uneasy conscience is that it? Come on Robbie.
Throw out those golden tones. Let them wing their way
across the empty sea. No that that sea's empty. Bloody
teeming that sea. Bloody sewage tank, that sea.

ROBERT:

Once a native maiden and a stranger met,
Underneath a blue Tahitian moon,
The stars were in her eyes,
Gardenias in her hair,
An' she vowed to care for ever.

JAMIE: Oh plaintive.

ROBERT:

Then one lonely day the stranger sailed away,
With a parting kiss that came too soon,
And now the trade winds sigh,
When ships go sailing by,
Underneath a blue Tahitian moon.

(*The light glows into evening.*)

JAMIE: Plaintive. Plaintive. Are those no tears I see in the wee

lady's eyes. Och flower. Come an' eat cous-cous wi' us
down the Casbah.

FERLIE: I can't.

JAMIE: Pretty wee flower like you shouldnie be alone on a night
like tonight. Come an' eat a big floppy fish wi' us down the
pêcheries. Drink the *vin de pays*, come back here a wee
touch tiddly an' commit adultery wi' me.

FERLIE: Really not.

JAMIE: The fish or the adultery?

(*He laughs. She doesn't.*)

Eh? Eh?

FERLIE: No. Really. Thank you.

JAMIE: Right if you don't fancy me. What about him? I'll be his
pander. Take a close look. He's got lovely markings. Some
women'd pay tae get their hands on him. To you. Nothing.
A freebie. On the house. Expense account meal at the Saint
George Hotel. Luxury in these socialist climes for those an'
such as those if you've got the pennies. Bamboo bird-cages
the size of small bungalows. Chateaubriand on the marble
balcony. An' a wee silver desert fox that'll come an' sit in
yer lap, waitin' for a pet an' lick you wi' its rough wet
tongue. An' you. You've a way wi' desert foxes haven't you
my lady.

FERLIE: What?

JAMIE: Look at him. See Robbie. Robbie can show you life.

FERLIE: My sister's . . .

JAMIE: Robbie's the best lover this side of Saudi Arabia. He'll
fan the heat of your desire an' give you a memory of an
Algerian night that'll warm the cockles of your clitoris for
the next fifty years.

FERLIE: Please don't.

JAMIE: A wee joke.

FERLIE: I don't like it.

JAMIE: Robbie. Robbie. I've gone too far. I've set the lady's
teeth on edge an' she's no a lady to tangle with. Is that not
right?

(*Pause.*)

FERLIE: What?

JAMIE: I'm sorry, sorry, sorry. I've a tongue that gets me deep
in trouble. I've a clever tongue. Clever, clever, clever.
(HOCINE *brings a tray of bottles of mineral water.*)
Moral rearmament. An' there. There. A woman girt wi'
stone. See her face. See it. A smile would crack that face.
(SUSAN *leans against a column and waits.*)
Blessings upon you. Blessings my child. Blessings.
Blessings.

HOCINE: I regret to have to tell you that we have no water for
the present. It is our hope that it will come back. Until that
time will you be so kind as to perform your ablutions in
mineral water.

JAMIE: Would you look at this.

FERLIE: Susan.

JAMIE: Jesus God. There's bloody bubbles in this. There's
bloody fizz in this. Washin' my bits an' pieces in this. I ask
you. I bloody ask you. (*All the time he's watching the sisters.
Watching and watching.*)

FERLIE: Susan?
(*Blackout.*)

SCENE 3

*In the room behind the balcony the shutters are closed. The light slats
through. The overhead fan is turning and the curtains blow. The
women tiptoe and whisper. The figure on the bed lies still.*

FERLIE: You didn't close his eyes.

SUSAN: I held him.

FERLIE: You should have closed his eyes. (*She moves over
towards the bed. She crashes into the rose de sable. It breaks on
the marble floor. It breaks into bits.*)
God. O God. God. Oh God.

SUSAN: Quiet.

FERLIE: God. God. God.

SUSAN: Quiet. Quiet.

FERLIE: That was a present.

SUSAN: We'll clear it up.

FERLIE: You bought that for me.

SUSAN: That's what we'll do.

FERLIE: That was a present you bought for me.

SUSAN: We'll clear it up. What the hell did you come out here
for.

FERLIE: He tried to rape me.

SUSAN: I bought you that to save you getting rouked. All the
tourists. They all come out here. Roses de sable. They buy.
That's what they buy. I bought you that.

FERLIE: I had to defend myself.

SUSAN: Aye.

FERLIE: Oh Jesus.

SUSAN: You defended yourself alright.

FERLIE: Look at his eyes.

SUSAN: I held him in my arms and he died.

FERLIE: There isn't a brush and shovel in this place. He's
lookin' at me.

SUSAN: Close his eyes.

FERLIE: Who was he?

SUSAN: I don't know.

FERLIE: Did he say anything.

SUSAN: No.

FERLIE: He must have said something. You can't just die an'
not say anything. So you can't. Who was he? You can't.
You can't. (*She closes his eyes.*) I'd give anything for a brush
an' shovel. He's not a poor man, this man.

SUSAN: Don't paw at him.

FERLIE: He's no poor wi' a suit like this.

SUSAN: Don't pull him about.

FERLIE: He'll be smelling soon.

SUSAN: Leave him be.

FERLIE: You're no squeamish are you? You? You've planted
bombs in public places. You canny be squeamish. He's no
in bad shape.

SUSAN: He's dead.

FERLIE: Considering.

SUSAN: Oh aye. Look at that sheet.

FERLIE: You'd think they'd have a dustpan and brush.

SUSAN: Shhhhhhhh.

FERLIE: I'm standing on all the bits.

SUSAN: Quiet.

FERLIE: We'll have to wash the sheet. There's no two ways about that. At the very least we'll have to wash it.

SUSAN: Ferlie.

FERLIE: I canny wash a sheet in mineral water. No a whole sheet. Susan. There's no enough mineral water in the world tae wash that sheet. What are we gonnie do?

SUSAN: I don't know.

FERLIE: What do you mean?

SUSAN: Eh?

FERLIE: You must know.

SUSAN: I don't.

FERLIE: This is your line of work.

SUSAN: We all end up here. All the clapped-out radicals. This is our pilgrimage.

FERLIE: You've to take care of me.

SUSAN: Black Panthers. Baader-Meinhof. Yesterday's terrorists. It's a good life here. And we've all got sisters. Aye, and mothers too. They marry each other the terrorists here.

FERLIE: Are you after sympathy?

SUSAN: No.

FERLIE: You made your bed.

SUSAN: What are we talking about?

FERLIE: You took your stand. You got on with it. Without reference to . . . You put your bombs in letter boxes. Jesus Christ. You couldnie even be original. You did it without reference to mother or sister. I'm no for violence. D'you hear me. I hate violence. You did it. You take the bloody consequences.

SUSAN: You live in compartments you. All neatly sectioned off. Nothing crossing the lines. You take your opinions off the supermarket shelves along with the nappies and the baby wipes. Look over there. That's your bed over there. Now you lie in it.

FERLIE: Remember Hogmanay.

SUSAN: Do you hear me?

FERLIE: You an' me. Wrapped in wur quilts. Peeking out the window. (*She reaches out to* SUSAN.)

SUSAN: What?

FERLIE: D'you mind that? An' all the folk.

> A good New Year tae ain an' a',
> An' mony may you see.

SUSAN: We'll have to get rid of him.

FERLIE: Oh God Susan did I do that? Have I killed a man? (*Pause.*) It wasnie me. It wasnie me. It wasnie the cough that carried him off. 'Twas the coffin they carried him off in.

(*Pause.* FERLIE *starts to giggle, then* SUSAN.)

SUSAN: What made the hearse horse hoarse?

FERLIE: What made the hearse horse hoarse?

SUSAN: The coffin.

(*The giggles grow and grow. Full-bellied laughter comes out of them, then goes.*)

FERLIE: Oh God I'm so hungry. I haven't eaten since . . . I haven't eaten. (*Beat.*) What I came out here for. I came out here to see you, that's all. I came out tae talk to you. I missed you. (*Beat.*) Chop an' chips I could eat. Mince an' stovies. (*Beat.*) How do we get rid of him Susan. I've got to get back to my family. They'll put me in the gaol. It's not my fault. This. I didn't ask him to . . . This. I've got to get home. Come on. Come on. You're my big sister. Help me.

SUSAN: That man down there. He knows.

FERLIE: No one knows.

SUSAN: He knows.

FERLIE: No one knows. D'you hear me? Do you? No one knows. We'll spend the rest of the day by the pool you an' me.

SUSAN: I've my work.

FERLIE: I'm your sister. Your sister's come to stay. You're spending time with your sister. D'you hear me? Do you?

SUSAN: Sh. Sh. Sh.

FERLIE: We'll eat. We'll laugh. We'll swim. That's what we'll do. When the night comes. At night. In the dark, when it's quiet. We'll put the body in your car. We'll be alright. No one'll see. No one knows. No one'll know. We'll take the body. Just you an' me. We'll drive down to the desert. The two of us. We'll take the body in the boot of the car. We'll bury him in the desert. We'll do that. That'll be fine. We can do that. You an' me.

SUSAN: I haven't got a spade.

FERLIE: Yes you have.

SUSAN: I haven't. I haven't.

FERLIE: I'll dig his grave with my hands if I have to . . .

SUSAN: Ferlie . . .

FERLIE: I'll get home.

SUSAN: Sh. Sh. Sh.

FERLIE: That's what we'll do. That's what we'll do. You bring the car. That's what we'll do. I came out here for a rest.

SUSAN: Sh. Sh. Sh.

FERLIE: You should have had me at your flat.

SUSAN: We'd 've been at each other's throats.

FERLIE: You should have got a doctor.

SUSAN: Cover him up.

(FERLIE *holds the covers.*)

FERLIE: You could have saved him.

SUSAN: Cover him.

FERLIE: You can do anything you want. You always could.

SUSAN: Come on.

FERLIE: You could have saved me. (*She prods at the body.*) Wake up. Wake up damn you. (*She prods at the body.*) I won't have you dead. (*She prods at the body.*) He'll wake up. I know he's gonnie wake up.

SUSAN: Cover him.

FERLIE: (*Touches his cheek*) He's that cold. His skin feels . . .

SUSAN: Please Ferlie.

FERLIE: He's small. He's much smaller than . . .

SUSAN: Please.

FERLIE: I didn't do this.

SUSAN: Cover him.

FERLIE: I'm Ferlie. You. D'you hear me? You. Ferlie. Wake up.

SUSAN: Pull the sheet up.

FERLIE: Look at him. He'd never have harmed me.

SUSAN: Come on.

FERLIE: I've murdered him.

SUSAN: Stop it. Cover him up.

FERLIE: God'll curse me, Susan. He's up there in the sky an' he'll curse me.

SUSAN: You're not some wee girl. Cover that man up.

FERLIE: You do it. (*Pause.*) You can't, can you? You can't do it.

(SUSAN *covers him. It takes her to do it.*)

SUSAN: There's no bogie man.

FERLIE: Aye there is.

SUSAN: Come here. (SUSAN *puts her arms round* FERLIE.)

FERLIE: Hold on to me.

SUSAN: It's alright.

FERLIE: Hold me.

SUSAN: I'll see it's alright.

FERLIE: Oh God Susan. (*Beat.*) I'm so hungry. I'm so hungry. (*Blackout.*)

SCENE 4

HOCINE *is behind the bar. He's clearing up. It's evening. There are fairy lights around the pool.* HOCINE *switches them on. In the garden stands a spade.* FERLIE *and* SUSAN *stand at the side of the pool in the light.*

SUSAN: There it's there.

FERLIE: John an' me. At home. We're so busy John an' me. He looks at me. He's cleanin' his teeth. I'm sitting on the lavatory pan.

SUSAN: See.

FERLIE: I get very constipated sometimes. 'Do you think,' he says. He says to me. 'Do you think the romance has gone out of our marriage?'

SUSAN: Distract him an' we can get that.

FERLIE: We canny just steal it.

SUSAN: What do you suggest?

FERLIE: Memories. That's what we've been living on John an' me. I came out here . . .

SUSAN: ' 'Scuse me I just need to dig a wee grave in the desert. Can I borrow your spade?'

FERLIE: It's not his spade. He's not the gardener. It's not the gardener's spade. That spade belongs to the hotel.

SUSAN: 'I've a dead body upstairs I just need to bury. I'll bring your spade back shortly. Thank you very much.'

FERLIE: 'Don't have sex before marriage. It's bad enough afterwards.' Remember Mum saying that? I came out here . . .

(SUSAN *starts to laugh*.)

What is it? What's wrong?

(SUSAN *goes on laughing*.)

What's so funny? There's nothing funny.

SUSAN: I thought. I always thought. Whatever happens in my life I will meet it with dignity. I will be dignified. Oh God. Ferlie. We'll steal that spade. That's just what we'll do. Ferlie.

FERLIE: You've not been listening to me, have you?

SUSAN: I've other things on my mind.

FERLIE: You never listen to me. I came out here to talk to you. I needed you. I wanted . . .

(*The shutters across Ferlie's bedroom window fly open with a bang*.)

SUSAN: Jesus.

FERLIE: Oh my God. The sun'll get in there.

SUSAN: There's no sun.

FERLIE: It'll get hot in there.

SUSAN: There's no sun.

FERLIE: He's exploded.

SUSAN: Eh?

FERLIE: Him. The gases in him.

SUSAN: What?

FERLIE: You know. He's exploded the shutters out.

SUSAN: It's the wind.

FERLIE: Yes.

SUSAN: We've a job in hand. Distract him.

FERLIE: Are you sure it's the wind?

SUSAN: Smile at him. Show him your winsome ways.

FERLIE: I thought you were above that sort of thing.

SUSAN: I may be. You're not.

FERLIE: I remember you in the long grass up the bank at the back of our house. In among the trees. You lyin' in the grass an' David McAllister standin' over you like a great big stookie an' you pullin' up your dress an' showin' him your knickers. You had a red cardigan on. Smilin' you were. Smilin' an' smilin'.

SUSAN: Go an' talk to the man. Talk to him. That's all. It's not a seduction we're after. We've one body to clear up an' bury. That's enough. Talk to him. I'm goin' for the spade.

FERLIE: I was polite last night that's all.

SUSAN: Talk to him will you?

FERLIE: We were brought up to be polite.

SUSAN: Get on with it.

FERLIE: You can't see it from my side can you?

SUSAN: If you'd been less polite last night we might not have a dead body on our hands. We need the spade.

(FERLIE *walks over and sits at the bar.* SUSAN *watches.*)

FERLIE: The dark comes quickly here. (*Silence.*) It's a long day for you.

HOCINE: Hmmm.

FERLIE: You'll be tired.

HOCINE: Hmmm.

FERLIE: It's a lovely country you've got here. I love your country.

HOCINE: What do you want?

FERLIE: Pardon?

HOCINE: A little brown boy. That is what you want.

FERLIE: Sorry?

HOCINE: You women. You come out here.

FERLIE: I'm a socialist.

HOCINE: Sex that is what you come out here for.

FERLIE: No. No. No. No. No. No. I came out here . . .

(SUSAN *starts to move towards the spade.*)
I came out here to find . . . It's a beautiful country. I've
dreamt of this country. I came out here . . .

HOCINE: You are a woman therefore . . .

FERLIE: I'm only making conversation that's all. Passing the
time of day. You were friendly enough this morning.
(SUSAN *catches* FERLIE's *eye. Shakes her head.*)

HOCINE: I am off-duty now.

FERLIE: I've no ulterior motive. Well. I'm not after your body
if that's what you think.

HOCINE: Lone women by this pool.

FERLIE: I've had enough of . . .

HOCINE: I have been . . .

FERLIE: . . . bodies.

HOCINE: Raped I have been.

FERLIE: What?

HOCINE: We have been.

FERLIE: I'm a very moral person.

HOCINE: Women by this pool.

FERLIE: I'm really not like that.

HOCINE: Women smiling.

FERLIE: It must be awful for you.

HOCINE: All the time smiling.

FERLIE: I've other things on my mind.

HOCINE: The way you smile at me.

FERLIE: I was brought up to be pleasant. Me. I was taught to
smile. 'A long face is a spit in the eye of God's bright
heaven,' my Mother said. 'Smile,' she said. 'Smile.'
Smiling's what I do best. I've had a lot of practice. It
doesn't mean . . . (*she snaps her fingers*) that. Mind it gets
things done. A smile goes a long long way. Even the
electricity board are susceptible to . . .
(*She sees* SUSAN *moving towards the spade. Gabbles on.*)
Mind I'd rather have passion. My life is singularly lacking
in passion. I've envied . . . Still I rub along. My sister's
. . . If we were all the same? What would life be if we were
all the same?

HOCINE: My brother . . .

FERLIE: 'Smile,' she said. 'Smile.'

HOCINE: My brother was a passionate man. He had trucks in the revolution.

(FERLIE's *watching* SUSAN. *Putting her body in between* HOCINE *and* SUSAN.)

He brought in guns in the trucks. A passionate socialist. A fighter. He looked at this country after the revolution. This is not socialism. He took his key. He locked his door. He took his wife, his children. My Mother. He went to Morocco. This is not socialism.

FERLIE: A gun-runner. A hero?

HOCINE: I have a picture in my mind. I have a feeling in my heart. There is socialism. I am a very patient man.

(FERLIE *shivers.* HOCINE *wraps a shawl round her . . . an Arab headdress.*)

Ten dinars.

FERLIE: What?

HOCINE: Ten dinars.

FERLIE: Yes. Yes of course.

HOCINE: My brother, he thought. Shoot them all. Bang. Bang. Bang. Bang. Socialism.

(SUSAN *has the spade.* ROBERT *materializes at her shoulder.*)

ROBERT: Gardening.

SUSAN: Christ.

(*He pats his guitar. Smiles.*)

ROBERT: Music?

SUSAN: Yes. Yes, of course.

(JAMIE *is shouting drunk.*)

JAMIE: Service. Service. Service. Service.

SUSAN: Jesus.

JAMIE: Gie us a drink there.

HOCINE: The bar is closed.

JAMIE: You're here. I'm here.

HOCINE: We are short-staffed.

JAMIE: Gie us a drink. Quisquavae. The water of life. Eh, my good woman. Good, good woman. We'll drink tae the good woman here.

Campbeltown Loch, I wish ye were whisky,
Campbeltown Loch, och aye,
Campbeltown Loch, I wish ye were whisky,
I wad drink ye dry.

HOCINE: Closed.

FERLIE: Ten dinars.

JAMIE: All your wee fiddles. You can keep yersel' goin' eh
Hocine. There might be children dyin' in the street. Eh?
Eh? but you're alright. Eh my son. Eh Hocine. Look at
that suit. Will you look at that suit. That suit. You wear
the label on the outside of that suit. Give us a feel o' that
material. A wee treat for my fingers.

(HOCINE *pulls back.*)

Suit yersel' man. Eh? Eh? Suit yersel'.

(*The shutters of Ferlie's room bang mightily.*)

Bring out yer dead. Bring out yer dead. (*He takes bottles
from his pockets. Empty half-bottles of whisky and lines them
up on the bar.*) All they dead men. (*Beat.*) I saw you. The
both of you.

FERLIE: What?

JAMIE: Him. Him an' you. Gettin' real friendly. My girl. My
married lady.

(*The shutters bang.*)

Light of my eye. Flower of my heart.

She lifted up her lovely head an' cried,
Madam. Miss Otis regrets,
She's unable to lunch today.

Know that one do you? Do you know that one?

Last evening down in Lovers' Lane she strayed,
Madam. Miss Otis regrets,
She's unable to lunch today.

Dance for us Hocine. (*Silence.*) I've fifty dinars says you'll
dance for us.

(*He puts the dinars on the bar. Beats his guitar like a drum.*
HOCINE *dances.*)

Aye. Come on. Come on my wee cock. Dance. Eh? Eh?

My namby-pamby. My wee pansy in yer sleek suit. Come
on wi' ye. Aye look at him. Look at him. Never say I don't
know how to treat the Natives. Putty in ma hands. It's a
lesson I've learnt frae the English. Long an hard I've learnt
it. Look at his eyes. Dance. Man. Dance. (*Beat.*) Aye. I see
you. I see you. There's violence in every one of us. Eh.
Hocine. Eh. My fine fellow. Ferlie here. Wee smilin'
Ferlie. Wee smilin' wifie. There's violence in Ferlie. Is that
no right?

(HOCINE *stops dancing.*)

I've no had my fifty dinars' worth, no yet son. Dance, man,
dance.

(*And* HOCINE *dances.* ROBERT *beats on his guitar.*)

Ferlie here. She's a good hard hand on her. Is that no
right? She bashes her kids. They know her when she's
riled. That right my lass. Eh Ferlie? Show me a kind
woman. Eh? Eh? Come on. Come on. See him. See him
bristlin' away there. You Hocine. Come on. Belt me.
That's what you want eh? What's stoppin' you eh my
bantam? You Hocine. Come on. Belt me. Eh? Eh?

(ROBERT *lets out an Arab woman's scream.*)

What did you do in the revolution? What did your Faither
do? What did yer Mother do? She's no the clean potato I'll
bet. Did she take off her veil? Did she? Did she? Did she
carry the bombs into the cafés? Did she kill? Did she? Did
she maim? Eh Hocine? Eh my man? Did she torture? Did
she? Did she? Were there children in the cafés? Were the
kiddies there? Did she blow them to pieces? Did she leave
them bleeding in the gutter? Did you watch her weeping
for the blood on her hands?

(*The shutter bangs and bangs.*)

Bring out yer dead (*Beat.*) Did she bath you? Did she put
you to bed? Did she kiss you? This Mother. This killer.
Did you see the pictures behind her eyes, the bloody
corpses of children lying cut up in a bombed café?
Freedom fighter. Liberator. Did you love yer Mother,
Hocine? Did you love her?

(HOCINE *stops dancing, faces* JAMIE, *looks at him, simply looks.* ROBERT *stops drumming on his guitar. In the silence the shutter bangs.*)

No my teeth. No these teeth. Cost a fortune these teeth. You canny get decent dentures on the National Health.

(*Quietly* HOCINE *speaks. Patiently he speaks. Putting on his jacket. Tidying the bar. A man in his place of work. In his own place.*)

HOCINE: You. Your kind. You come here. You patronize us in such a way . . . you seek to have us humble.

JAMIE: A hundred dinars I'll put down tomorrow night an' you'll dance to my tune.

HOCINE: We have fought for our beliefs. We have fought for our freedom.

JAMIE: Have you found it? Have you?

HOCINE: What have you done?

JAMIE: We're the same thing you an' me. Brothers for a' that.

HOCINE: We have laid down our lives. We have known joy. We have known despair. We have been comrades. We have stood and we have not . . .

JAMIE: For a' that an' a' that. I can get right under your skin.

HOCINE: I am soiled by you. Me. My folk. My country. I would like to see the last of you.

JAMIE: Night. Night.

HOCINE: I look forward to a day when you and all the people like you will go and not return, not ever return.

JAMIE: Night night my cock of the walk. My wee bantam. I'm done wi' you now.

(*Pause.* HOCINE *looks round.*)

HOCINE: You talk. That is what you do. I have listened to you talk.

(HOCINE *pulls the shirt cuffs down from his jacket sleeves and goes. Silence. All eyes are on* JAMIE. FERLIE, SUSAN *and* ROBERT *too, staring at him.*)

JAMIE: Aye you can look. You can all look. Scotland made me. Each one of us here. Big quiet Robbie. Big quiet man. An' Ferlie. Sweet smilin' Ferlie. An' you. Susan is it? Who the Hell are you? Scotland bore me. Sco-t-land. See Robbie. See Robbie standin' there. Robbie's a romantic. He's got this grand and glorious idea that ships can be built on the Clyde. Dangerous men romantics. He wants to open a shipyard. Open one? I ask you. I bloody ask you. Sco-t-land. I met an Englishman out here. Mark you this. Mark you this. I canny get a job at home. I cannot offer my skills to my native land. Not though they trained me. Not though I never want to leave its work-forsaken shores. This is his land. It's no mine. I'm a foreigner here an' I love my home. I'm in exile. Listen you here to my lament. (*Beat.*) 'Glasgow,' says my Englishman, says he to me, 'I had my chaps do some research in your country. Development Board offering empty factories free. That sort of thing.' (*Beat.*) The English. The way they speak. The English. It's horrible the way they speak. I'm out here I cry for my country sometimes. The butchers of Culloden Field live on in the heart of they bloody English. (*Beat.*) 'Factories for nothing. Not worth it. They told me. That's what my boys told me.' (*Beat.*) I come from a subject race. (*Beat.*) 'The average Scot has his council house and does not want to work.' (*Beat.*) They've rape in their bloody soul. (*Beat.*) 'It would be cheaper to build a factory from scratch in Kent and employ men with thirty-thousand-pound mortgages. They have to work.' (*Beat.*) Rape. Genocide. (*Beat.*) 'The Development Board chappie burst into tears.' (*Beat.*) Shoot the bloody English. Sco . . . t . . . land. Sco . . . t . . . land. Aye look at me. I see you looking at me.

> Last evening down in Lovers' Lane,
> She strayed. Madam
> Miss Otis regrets
> She's unable to lunch today.

(*The shutters bang and bang. Blackout.*)

SCENE 5

The beach. The stars twinkle and the moon shines off the sea.
FERLIE *and* SUSAN *are carrying the body over the sand.*
FERLIE: The day you skipped bail my Father cried. Do you

hear me? Out in his greenhouse. All on his own. I saw him through the glass. I saw him sobbing.

SUSAN: Quiet Ferlie. Hush now. Hush. Hush. Hush.

FERLIE:

> Hush my baby do not cry,
> And I will sing a lullaby.

I want my kids.

SUSAN: Move.

FERLIE: Oh my God.

SUSAN: What is it?

FERLIE: The scorpions. In this sand. In this sand. Scorpions.

SUSAN: No. No. No.

FERLIE: There is.

SUSAN: At the water's edge in the cool.

FERLIE: It's all cool.

SUSAN: Move.

FERLIE: I can't.

SUSAN: Come on Ferlie.

FERLIE: I've a tickle at my heel. I've a tickle goin' right up my back to my neck an' over my head.

SUSAN: Ferlie.

FERLIE: I've a scorpion on me.

SUSAN: There's nothing on you.

FERLIE: It's dark. You can't see. It's dark. I'll never get home.

SUSAN: I'll not see you in gaol.

FERLIE: Oh God he's heavy.

SUSAN: Come on.

FERLIE: We should have told.

SUSAN: You're girning Ferlie.

FERLIE: The truth.

SUSAN: You're a woman, that's the truth. An' you're white. You haven't got a chance. Move.

FERLIE: I can't. I can't.

SUSAN: Down behind the synagogue I remember you kissin' the boys.

FERLIE: It's crawlin' on me.

SUSAN: Six years old. All the boys lined up in a row.

FERLIE: What?

SUSAN: Step by step. Come on now. One by one . . . you kissed
them.

FERLIE: Did I?

SUSAN: One foot in front of the other. That's my good girl.
Long, long kisses you gave them. And sent them into *shul*.
Step by step. Down behind the synagogue in your grey
school uniform. Not so far to go now. Down behind the
synagogue where all the May trees grow.

FERLIE: I came out here.

SUSAN: Nine boys you had in a row.

FERLIE: I thought you could help me.

SUSAN: Kissin' them one by one by one.

FERLIE: Talk to me.

SUSAN: Smilin' you were. All the time.

FERLIE: You canny help me. Can you.

SUSAN: Not so far to go.

FERLIE: I live in the memory of those days. Those were happy
days. I'm frayin' all to bits, Susan.

SUSAN: You're alright.

FERLIE: The May trees and the scent of blossom. An' the wet
grass all shining in the sun. An' the peace. An' I'm
standing very still. When I grow up. When I grow up. I'll
live inside this when I grow up.

SUSAN:

Carolina moon keep shinin'.

FERLIE: Where is it Susan. Where is it?

SUSAN:

Shine upon the one who waits for me.

FERLIE: I'm all grown up now. Where is it?

(*They've reached the car.* JAMIE *and* ROBERT *are standing
there.* JAMIE *has the spade in his hand.*)

JAMIE: You'll be needin' this.

FERLIE: You're the devil aren't you.

SUSAN: What do you want?

JAMIE: It's a free country.

SUSAN: Go away.

JAMIE: We're a' Jock Tamson's bairns. He doesnie look well.

SUSAN: He's dead.

JAMIE: We all have to pay the piper. Where's he destined for?

SUSAN: The boot.

JAMIE: We're comin' wi' you. Him an' me.

SUSAN: You're not.

JAMIE: He'll can sit between us. Yer man there.

SUSAN: You don't set foot in my car.

JAMIE: An' if the law stops you? (*Beat.*) I know you. Oh aye. I know you. A woman of action. I know exactly who you are. (*Pause.*) Come on now. Use yer intelligence. Exercise that fine brain of yours. Is that not what they said about you? A woman wi' an analytic mind. Held on terrorist charges, you were. Conspiracy. Is that it? Is it? Is it now? A latter-day Joan of Arc you. Freein' the Scots from the weight of their oppression all on yer ain wee ownsome. No so very intelligent. The days for saints in armour are long gone. Did you not know that? These are the days of languor and acceptance upon us now. (*Pause.*) You're carryin' a dead body in the boot. Is that sensible? An' they'll stop you. The law'll stop you. Two white women drivin' into the night. They'll stop you, all in their green, wi' their guns an' their never a smile. They'll stop you. It's just no practical. We're with you. They see us wi' you. What have you got in the back of the car? You've three drunks in the back of the car. Poor weak men. Is that no right? My fine terrorist lady. Weak men. Come on woman. You canny look a gift horse in the mouth. We may not be much, me an' him, but we're all you've got an' you know it. You know it. Eh? Eh? Don't you know it. (*Pause.*) Aye.

(*Blackout.*)

ACT TWO

SCENE 1

*A road in the middle of the mountains. Great heaving shadows in
the darkness, moving in the torchlight and the light of the moon. The
car is stopped. The headlights shine out.*
SUSAN *sits at the wheel.* FERLIE *leans against the bonnet. And
smiles. And smiles.* ROBERT *has the dead body with its arms around
his neck.* JAMIE *has his guitar.*
The POLICEMAN *is standing by. Armed and ready.*

JAMIE:

> Hic a hooera
> A tac a hac a hooera
> Hic a hooera
> A tac a hac a hooera.

Have we no been to a party. Dance woman dance. What a
party have we been to.

> O wooera.

Waggle your hips for the nice gentleman Ferlie.

> Hic a hooera.

For are we no goin' into the desert tae bathe wur naked
bodies in the moonlight. *Comprendez monsieur.* We an' wur
friend here. If he's up to it by then for he's dead drunk.
Isn't he no. Dead drunk. You come along. Come on man.
Come along wi' us. For are we no men together. You an'
me. Are we no brothers. Under the uniform. Under the
skin. See her. See her. Do we no have a fine appreciation of
the female form, you an' me. See her. Fine example of
woman kind. *Comprendez.* Eh? Eh? You an' me. Eh? My
friend. My old compadre. Put up your carbine an' put up
your carbine. Eh? Eh?

Hic a hooera
A tac a hac a hooera.

Would you no just like a bit o' that. Flesh, eh? Soft flesh.
White flesh. Flesh you can taste. Eh my friend. Tasty.
Tasty. A right nice wee bit fluff that one eh.

How much is that doggie in the window?
The one wi' the waggly tail,
How much is that doggie in the window?
I do hope that doggie's for sale.

Bought an' paid for my man. Bought an' paid for an' all
wrapped up in its pretty packaging a waitin' to be undone.
Eh? Eh? (*He takes a bottle out of his back pocket, turns it
upside down.*) Would you look at that? Is that no a sad
thing? Have you ever seen a sadder sight than that? Does
that not bring the tears to your eyes?
(*The* POLICEMAN *puts his hand on* JAMIE's *arm. Pushes him
to one side.*)
What?
(*The* POLICEMAN *walks towards the dead man.*)
What he's packed away. I'll no tell you what he's packed
away. It's a wonder he's no deid frae it.

Cigarettes an' whisky an' wild, wild women,
They drive you . . .

Constitution of an ox that man there. Come wi' us. Come
wi' us now. Taste the wine of the flesh. (*He gets the
POLICEMAN round the shoulders.*) You've a beautiful
country here. I will say that. Mountain, sea, desert an'
song. What more could a man ask for? Eh? On a lonely
night. What more? On a night such as this. What more?
(*The* POLICEMAN *moves towards the dead man.*)
I've taken a liking to you. (*He swings the man round.*)
SUSAN: Jamie.
JAMIE: Compadre. Compadre.
ROBERT: Jamie.
JAMIE: Catch the scent of her. Can you? Can you?

ROBERT: Jamie.

JAMIE: We'll drink together yet. We'll taste the secrets of the dark, dark flesh. Eh compadre. My compadre. For that's it, is it no. That's the secret of womankind. Whatever the colour of their silk soft skins. They cover us with all darkness. They cloak us wi' mystery. They suckle us wi' black, black night.

(*The* POLICEMAN *begins to put his rifle down.*)

That's it my son. My good old son.

SUSAN: Jamie.

JAMIE: This is a good woman here. A good, good woman. There you are compadre. There, there, there you are.

ROBERT: Jamie.

JAMIE: His Master's Voice.

(*The* POLICEMAN *touches* FERLIE. *Moves his hand across her shoulder. Gently, gently lifts her dress.* JAMIE *moves away, back to the car. The* POLICEMAN *has his hands on* FERLIE's *hips, pulls her to him.*)

Douse the headlights.

(*No one moves.*)

Douse the bloody lights.

(SUSAN *switches off the headlights. The moon lights the faces of* JAMIE *and* ROBERT *and* SUSAN. *The moonlight falls on the dead man.* FERLIE *and the* POLICEMAN *are in the darkness. Silence.*)

SUSAN: Jamie.

JAMIE: It'll no take him long.

SUSAN: Oh God.

JAMIE: Quiet. (*Silence.*) Come on. Come on. Come on. Come on.

(FERLIE *comes back into the light and the silence. The* POLICEMAN *picks up his rifle. Pause.* SUSAN *guns the car engine.* ROBERT *swings the dead man into the car.*)

Dead to the world he is. The cracks of doom could ring an' you'd no wake him out of his torpor. Dead to the world an' quiet as the grave.

(JAMIE *has his arm round* FERLIE. *He's moving her into the car.*)

POLICEMAN: You are filth all of you. Your presence soils my
    land.

JAMIE: Aye an' you'll come down an' rut in the dirt wi' us. Is
    that no a fact? Compadre. You'll dip your stick in a white
    pot faster than . . .

FERLIE: Jamie.

JAMIE: Compadre.
    (*She lays her hand on his cheek.*)
    Aye. I'm wi' you. Ma wee hen.
    (*Blackout.*)

SCENE 2

*Past Bou Saada, the gate to the Sahara. Past Bou Saada by the
old film set, the wreck of the palace from* Samson and Delilah. *By
the old film set they stop the car. The moon shines on the rainbow
rocks of the Sahara, mauve and purple and deep, deep blue. The
stars shine on the yellow sand.*

The dead man lies flat out in peace. FERLIE *is staring at her
reflection in the mirror pool of the long-ago film.* ROBERT *leans
against the car, strumming his guitar.*

It's JAMIE's *turn with the spade. He's digging and digging. The
only sounds are his grunts and the sharp scrape of metal against sand
as the spade bites into the desert A far-off camel heaves its groans
into the darkness.* JAMIE *jerks upright, spade in hand.*

JAMIE: What the Hell is that?

SUSAN: A corporation bus.

JAMIE: Is that a joke? A wee joke there. She's cracking jokes
    now.

SUSAN: It's a camel.

JAMIE: I know it's a bloody camel. I know that.
    (*The camel groans.*)
    Somebody shoot that thing. It's in pain.
    (*The camel groans.*)
    Is that not a God awful sound? No that I've no heard
    camels. I've heard camels. Takes you aback. That. The
    whole of the bloody Sahara to choose from and you fetch us
    up by a herd of bloody camels.

SUSAN: One camel.

JAMIE: How do you know what's out there waitin' for us? There's a hundred thousand camels out there wi' a' their things jouncin' this way and that, chargin' down . . .

SUSAN: A wee camel.

JAMIE: Whose camel? Eh? Whose bloody camel? (*Pause.*) What did I say? (*Silence.*) I'm plum tuckered out. I've gone fifteen rounds wi' Mohammed Ali. Me. I'm that knackered.

SUSAN: Here. Give it here.

(JAMIE *passes over the spade.*)

JAMIE: My limbs are weak an' I'm cold. I'm that cold.

SUSAN: It'll be the shock I expect.

JAMIE: Don't you . . .

SUSAN: What? (*Pause. She starts to dig.*)

JAMIE: I did what I had to do.

SUSAN: Is that right?

JAMIE: You say nothing to me.

SUSAN: You set her up.

FERLIE: Quiet. Both of you. Please.

JAMIE: Come here.

ROBERT:

Will ye go, lassie go.

FERLIE: I'll not have you fightin' over me. I could've put a stop to it. I'm my own person. Don't you forget it.

ROBERT:

An' we'll all go together.

JAMIE: Let me put my arms around you. Come you here to me.

ROBERT:

Tae pluck wild mountain thyme,
All among the bloomin' heather.

JAMIE: I'm sorry.

FERLIE: What for?

JAMIE: I'm tellin' you. That's all.

FERLIE: It's a small price to pay. Isn't it. Is that not right? (*She sits down by the body.*) Zip-pe-de-do-da. A small price for freedom.

JAMIE: What the Hell is this place?

SUSAN: (*Leaning on the spade*) Delilah's palace. *Samson and Delilah*. Hollywood. Victor Mature and dancing girls. Lots of dancing girls. Right up your street. Eh Jamie? Am I not right?

FERLIE: Why are you helping me Jamie?

JAMIE: All the hallmarks of a Glasgow slum.

SUSAN: Chivalry.

JAMIE: Dark. Drear. Covered in slime an' it stinks a bit.

SUSAN: A bygone knight our Jamie.

JAMIE: The old slums. The Gorbals. They had class.

SUSAN: A romantic. Know what a romantic is. Do you?

JAMIE: Course it's a classless society we live in now.

SUSAN: A man who runs away.

JAMIE: Are you digging or what are you doing?

ROBERT: Gives me the bloody creeps.

(*They all look at him.*)

This place. (*He shrugs.*)

JAMIE: Here. Give it here.

SUSAN: It's not your turn.

JAMIE: Give it to me.

(*She holds on to the spade but she's shivering. Looking round her. Looking into the deep hole that makes the grave in the sand. Rubbing at her neck with her hand. Rubbing her face. Biting her lips.*)

What are you terrorist lady. Frightened of the dark an' ancient ghosts of Hollywood. They're no the ghosts that'll get you. Here. Here. Here's a dead man here. Take a good look. A good long look. You lot. Dreamers the lot of you wi' yer theories an' yer . . . good of the people. Here's death here. You take a good look.

ROBERT:

I will build my love a bower,
By the clear and crystal fountain.

JAMIE: (*Holds out his hand*) Give me the damn spade.

(*She gives it to him.*)

ROBERT:

> An' on it I will gather,
> A' the flowers o' the mountain.

FERLIE: What do you want Jamie?

JAMIE: Eh?

FERLIE: Is it payment you're after?

JAMIE: Och hen . . .

FERLIE: I mean . . .

JAMIE: I know fine what you mean. You an' him. Yon dead fellow there. I saw you the both of you.

SUSAN: We'd rather gathered that.

JAMIE: What the Hell is it wi' you? Sock it to me.

SUSAN: I despise you.

JAMIE: Christ Jesus why?

SUSAN: Are you gonnie dig?

(*He digs.*)

JAMIE: I yanked myself out frae the dirt in the gutter. I got hold of the wee short hairs on the back of my neck an' I pulled an' I pulled an' I . . . when I was fifteen I was goin' around wi' a sharpened steel comb lookin' for someone tae slash. I saw the error of my ways. All on my own. Not the polis. Not the Salvation Army. Me. Me. I was brought up on bread an' margarine and chips an' I can eat a steak au poivre wi' the best of them an' what's more I can cook it too. Don't you look down your long nose at me, my lass. I got an apprenticeship. Slums. I know slums. My crowd, the rest of them, they ended up in Barlinnie prison to a man. A man . . . I'm sayin' sorry to the lady.

SUSAN: Is that right?

JAMIE: Don't you come it. Death from the sky. That's you. Lady bloody Bountiful wi' a bomb in her hand. Fanny the Freedom Fighter. What do you know? Eh? No even the courage tae take yer medicine wi' yer so-called comrades. Eh? There they all are in their prison cells. Oh aye I know you. An' you're out here leadin' the life of Riley.

SUSAN: I don't want to be here.

JAMIE: All we poor chisellers out here in the real world.

SUSAN: I'm in exile.

JAMIE: An' we thank God for it. You an' all your kind. I'd lock you up for good an' a'.

SUSAN: You've got the answers. Bright eyes. Right then. Let's hear them. You're so much better than me. You tell me given the situation what we do. Do we vote? Is that it? Is that how we get out of it? Come on.

ROBERT:

Will ye go lassie go?

JAMIE: Take care of yer ain folk.

ROBERT:

An' we'll all go together.

SUSAN: How?

ROBERT:

Tae pluck wild mountain thyme.

SUSAN: I'll vote. I'll vote alright. And after I've voted. What then?

ROBERT:

All among the bloomin' heather.

JAMIE: Where do you get off wi' yer damn superiority?

FERLIE: Did you see?

ROBERT:

Will ye go lassie go?

JAMIE: You're a traitor to yer own bright cause.

FERLIE: Jamie.

SUSAN: Number one. That's who you're out for. You. Her. You're all the same.

JAMIE: The saint martyr standin' there. Jewels at yer neck. Rings tae yer fingers. Look at you.

FERLIE: Did you see me?

JAMIE: See yon dead man. I'm buryin' yon dead man. That's what I'm doin'. May his soul rest in peace.

FERLIE: Please.

JAMIE: Aye, hen, aye.

FERLIE: What did you see?

JAMIE: Freedom. I sold her for. Damn you, she's aye got her freedom.

(ROBERT *takes the spade*.)

FERLIE: Standing by the wall. Lookin' out to sea. He came at me. Did you see?

JAMIE: Och hen.

(ROBERT'*s digging*. SUSAN *jumps down into the hole and scrabbles at the firm sand on the bottom with her hands. Throws it out of the hole*.)

FERLIE: Did you see him at me?

JAMIE: Does it matter?

FERLIE: The first thing you saw.

JAMIE: You bending over him.

FERLIE: The first thing. The first thing.

JAMIE: That was it.

FERLIE: No.

JAMIE: I'm sorry.

FERLIE: You saw him. You did. You did.

JAMIE: Lassie. Wee lassie.

SUSAN: Let her be.

JAMIE: Hod yer noise.

FERLIE: You saw.

JAMIE: Whisht now. Whisht.

FERLIE: You saw it wasnie my fault.

JAMIE: I saw you bendin' over him. That's what I saw. That's all. Come here wee hen. Come here. I know what happened to you.

FERLIE: Why is he so quiet?

JAMIE: Whisht.

FERLIE: Is he wise. Is that it.

JAMIE: Come to my arms.

FERLIE: You're no wise. No you. You've got nothing to say.

JAMIE: Wee hen.

FERLIE: How can I go back?

JAMIE: You've lost yer bonnie smile.

FERLIE: I killed him.

JAMIE: It was a bonnie, bonnie smile.

FERLIE: Jesus, God I canny go back.

JAMIE: You're a wee smasher.

FERLIE: I canny stand at the cooker in my back kitchen. I killed a man. An' the school run, an' fish an' chips once a week on Friday. I canny touch my kids. A man's dead at my hands.

JAMIE: You're a wee smasher do you know that?

FERLIE: My husband's a nice man. A nice, nice man. An' my kids they're nice. An' me. I'm nice. I'm nice alright. They do say that about me. Ferlie, they say, she's nice. I've a wee fountain in my back garden. A wee pool an' a couple of carp. An' I'm nice. I came out here. I came out here. I've always had respect for you. No that I think you're right. I don't think you're right. Your commitment I envy. We had two miners to stay during the miners' strike that was. I made love to them, the two of them on the rug in front of the fire in my back room. We did it very quietly, the two of them an' me. That's a political statement. They needed a rest the pair of them. I gave them a good time. John was out an' we didn't wake the kids. I'm fibbing. Och I'm fibbing to you. I've been faithful to my nice husband all wur married life . . . I've been . . . I'm in prison where I live inside of me. The rules are all laid down for me an' I don't believe them, an' I can't change them, an' I can't stop living by them. I wish there was a God. It's all very difficult without God. There's the death of that man an' I canny work out whose fault it was.

SUSAN: It doesn't matter.

FERLIE: Aye it does. It does so. See me. Look at me.
(*They're all looking at her. She turns to* ROBERT.)
I'm in the street, collectin' for the miners. Smilin' an' smilin' I am. Cluttering up a Saturday morning. Front line suburbia. (*It's* ROBERT *she's talking to.*) An' the faces of the people when they pass me. Women in their tweeds an' their pearls an' their red lipsticks on their old mouths, all puckered up. An' the men in their good jackets going to the baker's for the new-baked bread. Old men. And once in a while. Now and then. A woman'll lift her hand to me. Like this. Fist all clenched. The women. No the men. (*She*

lifts her right hand across her body.) Raises her hand to me.
I'm a piece of dirt in her path. (*She makes a small movement
as if to hit.*) No that she hits me. Not her. Not them.
They'd like to right enough. I can see that in their eyes.
(*She moves her shoulder.*) Brushes me with her shoulder.
Accidentally on purpose. Just that wee bit too hard. Tut
tuts me. 'Look,' I'm saying inside. 'It's me. It's me.' An' I
keep the smile tight fixed to my face. An' they pass on, the
women. We don't see each other do we? Not really. Not
any of us. Do you not just love the smell of new-baked
bread? Say something. Go on. You must have something to
say.

    (*He leans on the shovel and looks. Just looks.*)

SUSAN: The light's chasing us.

FERLIE: I meant him no harm. (*She takes the spade from*
    ROBERT.)

SUSAN: Stars are fading.

    (FERLIE *starts to dig. Blackout.*)

SCENE 3

*Standing by the open grave. The four of them. The digging's done.
The body's in the grave.* ROBERT *has got the spade.*

SUSAN: It's gettin' lighter.

FERLIE: Is he deep enough?

JAMIE: The moon's up that's all. I've blisters on my hands.

SUSAN: For God's sake look at the sky.

FERLIE: The animals, they'll not get him.

JAMIE: What animals?

SUSAN: He's alright.

JAMIE: Camels do you mean?

FERLIE: I don't want him dug up.

JAMIE: They're vegetarians. Camels. Mind that doesnie
    necessarily make them pleasant. That's one of the myths of
    our time. I've never met a pleasant camel yet.

SUSAN: An' you've met a lot of camels.

JAMIE: I have. I have so.

FERLIE: He looks lonely down there.

JAMIE: I'll tell you a thing about camels. Every camel I've come across. Know what they've all got. They've all got . . .

SUSAN: The hump. Jesus Christ.

JAMIE: You've noticed.

FERLIE: The stars are awful bright.

JAMIE: One hump or two. Eh? Eh?

FERLIE: We canny just leave him here.

JAMIE: One hump or two.

SUSAN: Fill it in.

FERLIE: We can't leave him.

SUSAN: Oh Lord can we shovel the dirt on to this man? Can we cover him up? Can we do that? Can we finish this? Give me the damn spade. Give it to me. What are we waiting for? (*She starts to shovel the dirt on to the body in the grave. She works fast. Furiously. Until she's out of breath. And then she keeps on going.*)

JAMIE: Camel spiders you get in the desert so they do say. This size they are. (*He holds out his hands.*) A man's sleeping in the desert. Not a care in the world. Out under the stars. The romance of the desert. Wrapped in his burnous. Dreaming his dreams of peace. Along comes a camel spider. Going about his business. Climbs on to his face. Man doesn't feel a thing. Camel spider's attracted by the warm blood in him. Gets the smell of it. Like a magnet it is. Sticks his wee stinger intae the man's face. Pzz. Still the man doesnie feel a thing. Camel spider sits there waitin'. Waitin' for the juices from its sting tae have their effect. The stars shine down. Then the camel spider dips its head down tae the man's face an' starts tae eat. Eats its supper. An' the man sleeps on like a baby. The spider eats its fill, slowly, takes its time. An' when it's finished. Off it goes. Under the stars of the desert night. An' the man dreams on. Mind he's no sae very happy when he wakes up in the morning wi' half his face gone. Here, look. There's a shootin' star there. Over there. See. See.

ROBERT:

> Catch a falling star
> An' put it in yer pocket.

JAMIE: Aye. Nature. Eh?

ROBERT:

> Never let it fade away.

JAMIE: No now Robert. No now.
  (*Pause.*)

FERLIE: I don't know who he is.

JAMIE: Let him sleep. Leave him to his dreams. There's nae
  mair harm can come to him. Here . . . (*He takes the spade
  from* SUSAN, *holds it out to* FERLIE.) Go on.
  (FERLIE *shakes her head.*)

SUSAN: You started it. You finish it.
  (FERLIE *doesn't move.* JAMIE *shovels dirt down into the
  grave.*)

JAMIE: For a wee bit sex. A wee wee bit sex.
  (*He shovels and shovels. While* SUSAN *slumps exhausted. And*
  FERLIE *stares.*)
  A wee, wee, wee bit sex.
  (*And he goes on shovelling. Blackout.*)

SCENE 4

*A car engine turns and turns. The man is buried. The car coughs
and splutters in the empty night.* SUSAN's *turning the key. The car
dies.*

Silence.

JAMIE: There's never a bloody AA man when you want one.
  (*He opens up the bonnet.*) Jesus God woman. What the hell's
  this? Is this an engine or what is it. Cloth. Woman. Cloth.
  (SUSAN *brings him a cloth out of the car.*)
  See this. Look at this. Get your head in there. This is a
  woman's engine. The battery's clarty. The points are a'
  gunged up. There's nae water an' yer low on bloody oil.

SUSAN: Can you fix it?

JAMIE: I don't know.

SUSAN: You must know.

JAMIE: I'm the best god damn engineer on this bloody
continent. That's what I am. I'm no a bloody miracle
worker.

SUSAN: What's wrong with it?

JAMIE: Jesus woman. What's right with it. Have you petrol?
Come on now. Tell me the truth. Have you petrol in this
thing?

SUSAN: Of course.

JAMIE: There's no of course about it.

SUSAN: The dawn'll be on us. We'll be caught here.

JAMIE: If I'd a lifted the bonnet before we set out on this jaunt
I'd a stayed at home.

FERLIE: The wind's getting up.

JAMIE: A bloody shamal. That's all we need.

SUSAN: I didn't ask you to come.

JAMIE: Aye well I'm here now an' barring some bloody miracle
this is where I'll be staying an' I'll be layin' down my bones
here alongside that poor bugger over there. How could you
treat a peace of machinery like this?

FERLIE: The wind'll blow the sand from off him.

SUSAN: He's deep enough down.

JAMIE: If there's sand in the oil we're jiggered.

SUSAN: Hurry up.

JAMIE: I'm gonnie clean the plugs, I'm gonnie hold my breath
an' I'm gonnie hope.

SUSAN: Jesus.

JAMIE: An' I might even pray.

FERLIE: Hurry up. Hurry up.

SUSAN: Get on with it.

JAMIE: Please.

SUSAN: What?

JAMIE: Get on wi' it, please. It doesnie take much to be
pleasant to a man.

SUSAN: Don't be so stupid.

JAMIE: Please.

FERLIE: Please.

JAMIE: Aye I know hen. I know. (*Pause. He stands still.*)

SUSAN: For God's sake.

JAMIE: Hear that cry. On the wind. They reckon it calls to the people. An' out they go walkin'. Pit pat. Pit pat. Walk till they drop down. Lie there till they die. No me. Bloody ugly place this place. It's forgotten its humanity.

SUSAN: Jesus.

JAMIE: You try a man's patience.

FERLIE: We've got to go.

JAMIE: You know that an' I know that.

FERLIE: Oh God Susan.

SUSAN: Please.

(JAMIE *takes out the spark plugs*.)

I'm sorry for you.

JAMIE: We learn of womankind at wur mother's knee. Is that no right. My mother had a hard hand on her. I learnt the hard way. I knew my mother in her wrath. My mother had wrists on her . . . like . . . an' arms . . . I know women. My mother had five wains an' she brought us up hersel'. I know women. My Mother . . . oh aye . . . a strong woman my mother . . . what she longed for all her life through . . . know what it was eh? Do you?

SUSAN: What?

JAMIE: What she longs for yet. Eh? A man's arm round her. To shelter her.

SUSAN: There's no man's arm strong enough.

(FERLIE'*s at the grave, patting and patting at the sand, as the wind blows*.)

Hurry up. Hurry up. Please.

JAMIE: One day if you work at it. You'll make some man a fine wife. Mind. Yer no tae my taste.

SUSAN: You're poor souls. Men. Wi' that thing hangin' off in front of you. All vulnerable. Poor wee thing. What a piece of work. Call that design. It's no even safe an' it's certainly not sensible. Look at you. Exposed. God I feel sorry for men. Me. I can change. I can grow. I can bring forth life. Sustain it. My God I'm powerful.

JAMIE: Yer bloody innocent if you think you can do that all by yer own self.

SUSAN: The most you can do, the very most, is to grow a fuzz
of hair on your poor wee chin. It must be a worry that,
hanging off in front of you. My God I pity men.
(*Pause.*)

JAMIE: That's us got wur character. Robbie's learnt something.

SUSAN: Travel broadens the mind.
(*The engine starts.* JAMIE's *started it from under the bonnet.*)
Clever boy.

JAMIE: Your sister's singin' to yon hummock in the sand an'
we're a long way from home. Go on. Go an' tell her yon
dead fella's long past her lullabies. For a wee bit sex. Eh?
(SUSAN *walks down to the grave.*)
The wages of sin. (*He calls.*) Ferlie.
(FERLIE *looks up.* SUSAN *holds out her hand.*)

SUSAN: Come on.
(FERLIE *goes on sitting.*)
Christ Jesus. What now? Can we get going please?

JAMIE: Get a bloody move on.

SUSAN: Don't play the tragedy queen.

FERLIE: What?

SUSAN: We haven't the time. (*Pause.*) He won't get up and walk
out of there. It's finished.
(FERLIE *sits.*)

JAMIE: Jesus Christ girls.

SUSAN: He's going to start blowing the horn in a minute. Your
friend.

FERLIE: He's not my friend.

SUSAN: Well he certainly isn't mine. Move Ferlie.

FERLIE: I bought perfume at the Duty Free.

SUSAN: Look at that sky.

FERLIE: (*The words rattle out of her mouth*) My husband sits at
the end of the bed. After his bath this is. He sits at the end
of his bed an' he chips at the hard skin on his feet, chips at
it with a razor blade. 'Femme' I bought at the Duty Free
and I bought 'Mystère'.

JAMIE: What the hell's going on down there!

SUSAN: Come on.

FERLIE: No listen.

JAMIE: Move yourselves.

FERLIE: Please.

> (*Pause.* SUSAN *waits. Listens.*)
> I love my husband. He's an artist with a razor blade. Chips an' chips at the skin on his feet. An' when he's done he puts the razor blade back in its box. So the kids don't get it. An' he leaves a pile of hard dry skin that's slightly smelly on the carpet. He leaves it for me to clear up. We've a brown carpet. I bought *Vogue* in the airport. (*She watches* SUSAN. *Pleads with her.*) I had a gin and tonic on the plane.

SUSAN: Is that it?

FERLIE: I'm looking out down on the clouds an' I'm thinking. Castles in the air. Only with me it's men.

SUSAN: Well?

FERLIE: I dreamt of a man holding my hand in the moonlight. A man looking deep into my eyes.

JAMIE: Move.

FERLIE: A desert romance.

SUSAN: What do you want me to say?

FERLIE: Was that a sin? I need to know. There's a man dead here. An' I canny go back to my kids.

SUSAN: Aye you can.

FERLIE: I can't. I can't. Can I?

SUSAN: He attacked you.

FERLIE: I don't . . .

JAMIE: Come on. Come on.

SUSAN: He attacked you didn't he?

FERLIE: I don't know.

SUSAN: Jesus. You know. You know.

FERLIE: Yon policeman in the night. Did he attack me? How can I go home?

JAMIE: Robbie's getting impatient. This car's gonnie pack up. Robbie's a wild man when he's roused.

SUSAN: Come on.

> (FERLIE *gets up.*)

FERLIE: Do you think he's got a wife waiting for him? Or a mother even.

SUSAN: Get into the car.

FERLIE: Some wee man out for a bit nookie.

JAMIE: Jesus God for a moment there I thought we were gonnie see Robbie in a temper. Still waters run deep. Isn't that what they say? See Robbie. There's Robbie. What you see is what you get. There's nothing dishonest about Robbie. Is that no right son? Are we set?

(SUSAN *grabs* FERLIE's *wrist.*)

SUSAN: Aye we are.

JAMIE: That's nice. That's very nice. The age of miracles is not yet gone. God's in his Heaven and the moon shines down. (*He holds the door of the car open.*) Right then. (*Blackout.*)

SCENE 5

FERLIE *is standing at the edge of the sea in her bare feet. The hotel's behind her. The sheet's dangling from her hands. It's early, early morning.*

SUSAN: You've all my sympathy. Now pack your bags and go home.

FERLIE: You're a hard woman.

SUSAN: What do you expect?

FERLIE: A bit of love.

SUSAN: I love you very much. Now get off the beach. You're making a spectacle of yourself.

FERLIE: Is that all I get?

SUSAN: What do you want?

FERLIE: Put your arms round me.

SUSAN: You're in your bare feet at the water's edge where the scorpions are.

FERLIE: Are you frightened what people'll think?

SUSAN: You're responsible for us. Jamie and Robbie who helped you. And me. I'm already in exile. Where do I go from here. There's Hocine up there doing his work at the pool. You put a smile on your face and get off this beach. We're depending on you.

FERLIE: (*Sings wildly*)

He used to sing

Remember this

Raggedy music to the cattle as he swings

Dad used to sing this

Back an' forwards in the saddle of a horse
SUSAN: Have your nervous breakdown when you get back home.
FERLIE:

Down in the desert where the bad men are,
An' the only light is the evening star.
SUSAN: Ferlie.
FERLIE:

The roughest toughest man I know is
Ragtime Cowboy, dirty old cowboy . . .

Come on you remember.
SUSAN: Did you ever see such a view?
FERLIE:

He's a hifalutin' rootin' tootin' shootin'
Son of a gun from Arizona
Ragtime Cowboy.

See when you were in the dock Susan.
SUSAN: There's blue. And then there's more blue. God must be
in his Heaven.
FERLIE: You didn't smile once. Your face didn't move. What
was going through your mind.
SUSAN: Look out there. What do you see?
FERLIE: What were you thinking?
SUSAN: Blue.
FERLIE: You're awful pretty when you smile. You'd have won
their hearts with a smile. You could have been anything
you wanted in this life.
SUSAN: Are you looking?
FERLIE: All the photographers. You could have had them all on

your side. After all you never killed anyone. In the end.
One smile. And you cared. We could all tell that. If only
you'd smiled.

SUSAN: I don't like spiders.

FERLIE: What do you see out there?

SUSAN: We needed someone on the outside. The organization.
To keep it going. I had to run.

FERLIE: That's a lie.

SUSAN: We drew lots.

FERLIE: What do you bother lying to me for?

SUSAN: You're trailing that thing in the sand. Come off the
beach.

FERLIE: I bet my face has changed. I must have lost so much
weight. You canny kill a man and end up with the same
face. You canny sell your body . . . D'you know I haven't
eaten since the plane. That's a long, long time ago. I'll look
like I've been to a Health Club. I could go a piece of fish.
Is there really so much shit in that sea. A piece of dried
fish.

SUSAN: God stop wittering.

FERLIE: I'm getting myself in order.

SUSAN: Will I carry you up the beach. Will I do that? See him
up there. Hocine.

FERLIE: Do you have a good life here. Do you?

SUSAN: Come on. Come on.

FERLIE: With your good job. And your flat. Apartment. Have
you friends?

SUSAN: He's looking down here.

FERLIE: Are you happy? Are you at peace?

SUSAN: Please God Ferlie. Get off the beach.

FERLIE: Do you think of us back home? Do you miss home?
Do you think of your comrades inside the gaol? Do you live
inside your memories?

SUSAN: You'll blow the whole thing.

FERLIE: Do you want to go home? Do you? Do you?

SUSAN: Quiet Ferlie.

FERLIE: Do you look out from the balcony of your flat? Do you
hate the streets you're looking on? An' the men an' their

absinthe in the cafés. I know you oh aye. You can't get
away from me. I'm your history. See me back home. I face
things and I accept. I know you for the coward you are.
Why did you run away? Eh? Why did you Susan? Answer
me.

SUSAN: Here?

FERLIE: Aye. Here and now. See him up there. Maybe I want
to blow it. Give myself up. Let someone else take the
responsibility for me. Maybe that would be easier. What do
you think Susan? There he is. See him. See him.

SUSAN: I was in the prison.

FERLIE: The truth.

SUSAN: Take what you get. I owe you nothing.

FERLIE: I'm your sister.

SUSAN: I was on remand. We were waiting for the bail hearing.
Jackie and Clara . . . They got down to it. Classes they
organized. Discussion groups. For the women. I was cold.
No that it was cold in there. It wasnie cold. I was
shivering. Ma brought me a cardigan. I held it tight round
me an' I didn't let it go. They talked an' talked. Jackie and
Clara. They were laughing. I couldn't see the funny side of
it myself. They were excited. Jesus.

(*She starts up the beach away from* FERLIE. FERLIE *watches.
Stands still. Waits.* SUSAN *comes back. Continues.*)

Never a silence. There was no quiet in that place. When
Ma and Pa mortgaged the house and I got out on bail I
couldn't sleep. Nightmares I had wi' my eyes wide open. 'I
don't care how you do it,' Ma said to me. 'You get out of
this land. I'll not see a daughter of mine languish in the
gaol.' I ran away. I'm a coward. Now we've both told the
truth. Now we've judged each other right enough. For if
I've failed at least I tried. Reaffirmed our own
righteousness. And I might try again. For I don't believe in
lying down and . . . what? Accepting it? Is that what you
said? Is it? Is that what you did? Here? We make our fate.
The one and the other. Why the hell would you accept
oppression? You get your courage up and you protest.
However you can. And if no one listens you throw a bloody

bomb. You accept oppression and you condone it. Tacitly.
The Politics of Apathy. Now can we get off the beach.

FERLIE: You can't hurt people.

SUSAN: I didn't start it.

FERLIE: You're my own sister.

SUSAN: Tttt.

FERLIE: (*Smiles, wheedles*) We're a fine pair.

SUSAN: I can't grant you absolution.

(*The smile disappears from* FERLIE's *face. It doesn't come
back.*)

FERLIE: I'm not asking you to.

SUSAN: Pick up that sheet. (*She walks up the beach.*) It's trailing
in the muck.

(*Blackout.*)

SCENE 6

By the swimming pool. SUSAN's *leaning against the wall, waiting
for* FERLIE. HOCINE's *at the bar. He's stacking bottles of mineral
water.*

JAMIE: All over I washed mysel'.

SUSAN: Did you?

JAMIE: Bloody carbonated water. Eh? Where that didnie fizz.
Away on up there. Wash yersel'. Gie yersel' a thrill.

SUSAN: What?

JAMIE: Are you deif? Know what you could do wi'? I know
what you could do wi'. You could do wi' a good . . .

SUSAN: What?

JAMIE: They've closed off the pool. Nae mair water. Canny
have the holiday-makers catching cholera. No that there's
many holiday-makers. The scorpions see tae that. Keep the
numbers down. Eh Hocine. Eh. The scorpions keep the
numbers down, aye, an' the price of the whisky. (*Pause.*)
After all we've been through the gether do you not think
you could be a wee bit nice. I mean. I'm not asking you for
your friendship. I wouldnie be so bold. A wee smile.
(*Pause.*) We're goin' home. Thought you'd want tae know.

Robbie an' me. We're a team see. I'm the mouth an' he's the trousers. You canny break up a team.

> Westering home an' a song in the air,
> Light of the Isles an' it's goodbye to care.

I want my ain folk. I wannie see the clear bright light fallin' frae a Scottish sky on tae the fag ends floatin' in the gutter by a Glasgow tenement. I'm homesick. A' this sun, sea an' sand. I wannie stand at a Celtic football match wi' ma feet soaked through frae the piss on the terraces, half strangled by a length of soggy toilet roll. Wet strength. Know why I helped her, your sister? Her lovely, lovely voice an' her wee lassie's smile. I know what you're thinkin'.

SUSAN: What?

JAMIE: You canny kid me.

SUSAN: I wouldn't try.

JAMIE: You think I'm gonnie sing for my supper when I get home. You know talent when you see it. Am I not right?

SUSAN: Aye.

JAMIE: No. No. No. No. No. I'm gonnie be a rich man when I get home for the British government has a scheme. Self-help. You put up a thousand. They give you two. The small business. Is that no fine: Robbie an me six thousand pounds we'll have between us. We're gonnie join the ranks of the self-employed. Respectability. The brew'll no see us. Forty quid a week each for a year. Riches eh? We're gonnie open a shipyard. The hammer's ding dong eh? We're gonnie buy back a' they patterns that were sold tae the Japanese that now the Koreans have. We're gonnie buy them back out of our six thousand pounds. A shipyard on the Clyde. For is there not a war on the Gulf. I'm an opportunist. Eh? There's money in ships.

(FERLIE *comes down*.)

ROBERT:

> As I sailed my ship across the water.

JAMIE: A golden opportunity.

SUSAN: You look fine.

JAMIE: Aye you do. You do that.

ROBERT:

When to Hawaii I said goodbye.

FERLIE: I've got my case.

JAMIE: I can just see you in Largs.

FERLIE: Thank you for your help.

JAMIE: You'll set Largs alight.

FERLIE: I don't know what I'd have done without you.

JAMIE: Pity you didnie have the time for a suntan.

ROBERT:

All the world seemed sad an' still as if . . .

JAMIE: We're goin' wursels. Tomorrow we're goin'.

ROBERT:

It saw my grief an' heard my cry.

JAMIE: Pity you couldnie have waited. We could have travelled
the gether. Companions on the way. Friends to the last.

ROBERT:

Farewell to thee.

FERLIE: Well.

(FERLIE *goes over to the wall where* SUSAN *is. And they talk,*
SUSAN *and* FERLIE. *Gently. And as they talk* ROBERT *sings,*
quietly, behind them.)

SUSAN: We used to have fun together didn't we when we were
kids.

FERLIE: Now an' then.

ROBERT:

Farewell to thee . . .

FERLIE: I'm no gonnie tell any of them what happened.

ROBERT:

My passion flower for whom I long in vain.

FERLIE: Look at me. I'm the same. (*She isn't smiling.*)

ROBERT:

One fond farewell . . .

FERLIE: People have had worse secrets.

ROBERT:

And faithful we will be.

FERLIE: You've not to tell.

SUSAN: Go on home. Go back to Largs. Look out your windows and you'll see the sea.

FERLIE: I'll live the way . . .

SUSAN: Get on back to your cosy life. Go on. Hold hard to it. Pretend. You've had years of practice.

FERLIE: What does that mean?

SUSAN: Grip on to it with all your might and main. Though you're shaken to the core. For it's slipping away. Bit by bit. They're chipping away at it. Hold on hard. Sooner or later you'll get to where I am.

JAMIE: Eas-y. Eas-y.

FERLIE: I love you. You know I do.

SUSAN: Keep your head down Ferlie. Husband your resources. The flak's flying.

(JAMIE *watches* FERLIE.)

FERLIE: Don't you come back. D'you hear me? Don't you ever come back. I'll turn you in if you come back.

SUSAN: Will you?

FERLIE: You'd not come in peace.

(SUSAN *leans on the wall looking out into the blue.* FERLIE *leaves.*)

JAMIE:

Wi' a hundred pipers an' a' an' a',
A hundred pipers an' a' an' a'.

Swing those hips. Go on, wee wifey. Off you go now.

We'll stop an' gie them a blaw, a blaw,
A hundred pipers an' a' an' a'.

One, two, three, four. Go on ma hen.

(HOCINE *sits down in a chair at the table. He puts his feet up. He has a bottle of beer and a glass. He opens the beer. It fizzes over his hand. He licks the foam off his skin. Pours the beer into the glass. Blackout.*)